PROMISE AND PROTECT

BOOK TWO IN THE HEROES OF EVERS, TEXAS SERIES

LORI RYAN

OTHER BOOKS BY LORI RYAN

The Sutton Billionaires Series:

The Billionaire Deal

Reuniting with the Billionaire

The Billionaire Op

The Billionaire's Rock Star

The Billionaire's Navy SEAL

Falling for the Billionaire's Daughter

The Sutton Capital Intrigue Series:

Cutthroat

Cut and Run

Cut to the Chase

The Sutton Capital on the Line Series:

Pure Vengeance

Latent Danger

The Triple Play Curse Novellas:

Game Changer

Game Maker

Game Clincher

The Heroes of Evers, TX Series:

Love and Protect

Promise and Protect

Honor and Protect (An Evers, TX Novella)

Serve and Protect

Desire and Protect

Cherish and Protect

Treasure and Protect

The Dark Falls, CO Series:

Dark Falls

Dark Burning

Dark Prison

Coming Soon – The Halo Security Series:

Dulce's Defender

Hannah's Hero

Shay's Shelter

Callie's Cover

Grace's Guardian

Sophie's Sentry

Sienna's Sentinal

For the most current list of Lori's books, visit her website:
loriryanromance.com.

CHAPTER ONE

W*ow. Don't hold back, Dad. Tell him what you really think.*

Katelyn Bowden leaned her head back against the icy tile wall of the hospital corridor and listened to her father and Sheriff John Davies argue. The hallway reeked of pine-scented cleaner, a smell that had always set her on edge.

Katelyn gritted her teeth. Her father was dying. She'd come home to be with him during his last weeks—maybe months if they were lucky—and now that she was here, he wanted to send her away. That was nothing new to Katelyn, but her cheeks heated at the thought of John hearing this from her father. Humiliation was becoming an all-too-common feeling for her lately.

"Of course I called her, Alan. You're in the *hospital.* Why wouldn't I call your only daughter and tell her to come home?" John asked and Katelyn wasn't surprised by the confusion in his voice.

Katelyn had heard her father's opinion on her coming home before, albeit a gentler version. She knew exactly what he would say. He probably hadn't ever shared his thoughts on the topic with John, though. John probably believed Katelyn stayed out of Evers, Texas—her father's hometown—by choice. People here couldn't possibly understand her relationship with her father. The only thing the people of Evers saw was a daughter who never came home. They had no idea why.

Katelyn frowned. Her father didn't *exactly* keep her at arm's length. Well, he did and he didn't. It was complicated. He was loving and caring in his own way with her. Throughout her entire childhood, he'd rarely missed one of his monthly visits to her in Austin, and as sheriff of a large portion of the Texas Hill Country, that was saying something. When he was with her, he doted on her. He simply didn't want her here, in his world. Katelyn had learned at an early age she wasn't ever going to be allowed to come home.

Her father's tone was harsh and unyielding as he spoke to John, drawing her back to the present. "You send her away, John. You tell her you made a mistake. She...she doesn't need to see me like this. I'll go see her when I'm feeling better."

Ah, a new argument. Now her father could say he didn't want her to see him in his current condition. There were some advantages to being on your deathbed, after all.

Katelyn knew if she walked in the room, her father would soften. He'd cajole and persuade instead of demand and order. He'd tell her she should be in Austin, where

2

she'd grown up with her aunt. He'd say she needed to stay near her studio for the sake of her art, be near the gallery that sold her work.

This time was different, though. Katelyn wasn't going back. She would tell him she already had another artist ready to sublet her studio and she planned to put her condo on the market. She would tell him it was too late to go back. She hadn't had time to pack much, but she would hire someone to pack the rest of her things and have them sent in the next week or so. Whether her father liked it or not, Katelyn was coming home to Evers.

Of course, neither John nor her father knew she had another reason for being in town. She wouldn't tell her father the whole story. He didn't need to know she'd been mortified to discover the man she'd been dating was hiding a wife and newborn infant from her. Or that her so-called friends simply shrugged when she told them and said they thought she knew. Katelyn wasn't sure whether it said more about her friends that they thought she knew but didn't care, or more about her. Why would they think she would do something like that? That she'd be that kind of person? When the call had come from John telling her how sick her father was, Katelyn had grabbed at the chance to walk away from all the mess and start over.

The door to her father's room opened with no warning and John came storming out. He pulled up short when he spotted her, and she could see the pity on his face when he realized she'd been listening to their argument.

"Katelyn, I..." He reached out a hand, but Katelyn stepped away, crossing her arms over her chest.

"Have you had an update from his doctor? Do they think I'll be able to take him home soon?" she asked, putting the conversation firmly in the realm she wanted. She wasn't about to discuss her relationship with her father with anyone—least of all John Davies.

She had started hearing about her father's Golden Boy when she was twenty-two and he'd come to work for her father, who was sheriff at the time. Her father couldn't stop talking about the man who would take over his department when he decided to retire. About the man who had become more than someone he mentored. The man who was like a son to him.

When she met John two years later on one of her rare trips to Evers, nothing John had done had been able to make it past the grudge she carried for him. By the time Katelyn met John Davies, she'd been firmly past the point of ever seeing him the way any other woman might. His golden blond hair and mesmerizing eyes might have captured most women's attention. Of course, she noticed he was tall and built like a tank. A very well-muscled, armored tank with a six-pack to die for and sinewy arms that could make a girl melt. But, she didn't respond to his natural good looks or his ready, dimpled smile. She didn't care if he flirted with her or turned on that charm that seemed to come so easily to him. Katelyn had seen John through eyes tainted with the strain of her father's desire to keep her out of his life.

She and John had continued to see one another from

time to time over the years. He'd come for dinner when she visited her father, and was always open and friendly with her. If John noticed her dislike of him, he never brought it up. But, the resentment on her side remained.

Standing in the hospital corridor with him now, Katelyn was shocked to find she *wanted* to let John comfort her. She wanted to let him hold her and tell her everything would be all right, that her father would be well again, even though she knew that wasn't true. So she reverted to what she did best. Katelyn shoved her feelings and emotions down, swallowing them before they could surface to where she'd be forced to face them. She looked at John with what she hoped was a blank expression and waited for him to fill her in on her father's medical status. The faster she found out what was going on, the sooner she could see her father and get home to deal with, in private, the emotional turmoil that was threatening to take over.

"Kate," John tried again.

"Katelyn." Oh, she knew she was being unacceptably rude, but she didn't want this man's pity. Didn't want it and didn't need it. "I can go find his doctor, if you don't remember all the details."

John leveled her with one of those looks he seemed to reserve only for her. The look that said he was simply patronizing her. The look that said he could read every thought and every emotion. How she hated it when he gave her that look.

"All right," John said slowly. "Why don't we grab a cup of coffee in the cafeteria, and I'll fill you in."

Katelyn didn't move to follow him. "I'd prefer to speak here and then go see my dad, John. I'm tired. I've just driven four hours, and I want to visit with him and then get settled in at home." There was that word again. *Home.*

So absurd, really. Her father's home in Evers hadn't been her home in years. Decades, really. Not since she'd been sent away when she was four years old. Not since her mother's murder.

"Fine," John said with a clipped nod. "The cirrhosis is as advanced as they thought it was when I called you earlier. There's no reversing the damage to his liver. He's not eligible for a transplant because he's flat out told his doctors he has no intention of giving up alcohol. He's got six months, tops. Most likely, a lot less."

Katelyn swallowed and tried to keep her face an even mask, showing little emotion, but she had to glance away from John and blink back the tears that were pushing their way out. How had her father hidden this from her?

Her voice turned to a whisper, even though she tried to put the strength of the anger she was feeling behind her words. "How did this happen, John? When...?" Katelyn looked down and gathered herself before meeting John's eyes again. "Why didn't you tell me he was drinking this much? How could you let him do this?"

She saw the wave of guilt hit John's face, and she felt bad for a moment before she managed to draw up her anger again. He should have told her. If he wanted to be a son to her father so damned much, he shouldn't have stood by and let this happen.

"I'm sorry, Katelyn. At first, none of us knew it was so bad. Once we figured it out, well, there didn't seem to be any way of stopping him, and honestly, we never thought things would get so bad so quickly. The doctor thinks he may have had an underlying medical condition that caused the cirrhosis to advance faster than it would have otherwise, but they just don't know for sure, yet."

His voice trailed off as though he didn't know what else to say, and Katelyn knew John didn't have any answers for her. Her father had been forced out of office two years ago when his opponent in the election for sheriff ran a malicious campaign in a bid to win. He had claimed her father was too old to perform his duties any longer, harping on his age again and again. The campaign had gotten downright ugly and her father had eventually stepped down rather than lose. He asked John to run in his place, believing it was the better thing to do for his constituents. John was young enough and had plenty of respect in the community to win the election without breaking a sweat, but retirement had turned out to be way too hard on her father. Retiring without finding her mother's killer...well, that had been more than he could handle. At least without turning to drinking, apparently. And, drinking heavily, it seemed.

"Fine," Katelyn said, mirroring what John had said only a moment before. She didn't have much fight in her right now.

"There's more, Kate," John said quietly. He moved closer to her in the hallway and looked around them before speaking. "I didn't want to mention this on the phone, but your dad's been confused lately."

She stared at him, not understanding. "What do you mean, confused?"

"He's experiencing some dementia. They're not sure yet if it's a result of the liver disease or if it's something entirely separate like Alzheimer's, but he's having episodes."

"Episodes?" She frowned. She was so used to her father being sure of himself. Confident that he was right all the time. Much like the man standing in front of her now. John was always in control, always in charge.

Katelyn shut her eyes for a moment, trying to rein in her emotions. She would *not* cry in front of this man. She took a deep breath before opening her eyes.

"I don't understand." She couldn't picture her father confused or unsure, despite what John said. "What kind of episodes?"

"He doesn't always know who I am when I visit. Or he knows who I am, but he forgets the year. The other day, he thought he was still sheriff and I was his deputy. He thought he'd been injured and that's why he was in the hospital. He gets frustrated, angry, when he can't remember things," John said.

She nodded, feeling like she was losing the last piece of her family. Wait, she *was* losing the last piece of her family. Her mother was gone. Her aunt, too. Now, her father. ...

"You need to be prepared, Katelyn. Some days, he may not know you," John said, his voice low and almost apologetic.

She cleared her throat and raised her chin to deflect the too-sympathetic look in his eyes and ward off the hot tears that threatened to fall. "Anything else?"

John shook his head. "No, that's it. The doctor said he'd tell us tomorrow whether they'll recommend discharging him or whether they want to keep him here longer. He said we could talk then about hospice options."

She had the bizarre realization that everyone here probably thought nothing of John Davies being involved in her father's care and any decisions that had to be made. It was clear the doctors and nurses had no problem giving him information and asking him to make decisions, federal privacy regulations be damned. Apparently, small town tradition could override even the most stringent of laws. Did they even think twice about the fact that *she* was Alan Bowden's flesh and blood while John was just...?

What was John? Surely not just someone her father worked with. But, he wasn't family either. She wouldn't accept that. And she wouldn't let the nurses and doctors act as if he were family. She'd tell them tomorrow that John did *not* have authority to make decisions or even receive private information, for that matter.

"I'll speak to them tomorrow."

John eyed her with an expression she couldn't quite read. "He'll need twenty-four-hour care if he comes home. I can help, Katelyn."

"No need. Thank you for calling me, John. I can take it from here." Katelyn turned and shoved open the door to her father's room. Time to face the man who'd sent her away twenty-four years ago and certainly wasn't happy to see her back.

JOHN SAW the flash of anger in her eyes and watched as Katelyn pushed open the door to her father's hospital room, her face set and resolute. She'd always been strong. There was determination and strength evident in everything Katelyn did. But he'd never seen her quite so angry, quite so stubborn.

He had suspected she would resist his help. He wasn't exactly high up on Katelyn's list of favorite people. But Alan Bowden had saved him years before. He'd somehow taken a man who had no reason to live, who had demons chasing him clear from New York City to Texas, and he'd brought him back to life. John owed Alan for that. He owed him everything. And he'd be damned if he'd let Katelyn shove him aside when the man who'd saved him from himself years ago lay dying in a hospital bed. She might not like him—even more now that she blamed him for letting her father drink—but she *was* going to have to deal with him.

He turned and walked down the long hallway toward the parking lot. The hospital was ten minutes outside of Evers, on the highway leading to Livingston Falls. He'd spent the whole day at the hospital, so he planned to swing by his office and check in with his deputies before heading home for the night. As John pushed through the exit door, the radio that lay on the left shoulder of his tan uniform crackled.

"Sheriff, you there?" Berta Silvers, the craggy-voiced dispatcher asked.

Roberta Silvers was most likely in her late sixties, although there was some dispute as to her actual age since she'd been celebrating her fifty-fifth birthday for at least the past ten years. Years of smoking left her sounding like a bullfrog trying to sing opera. Berta was an indispensable member of his staff, and one of a team of people who helped him run the sheriff's office in Evers. As sheriff, John had a whole host of duties, including overseeing the county correctional facility and prisoner transfers within the county. Together, everything often left him running on nothing more than fumes.

On top of it all, since Evers had always been too small to have its own police force, John was contracted to provide local law enforcement services for the town. Berta was not only his dispatcher; she was also largely responsible for keeping the local office running smoothly.

John keyed the large button on the side of his radio. "Yeah, Berta. What is it?" he asked.

"Danny wants to know if you're coming back in to the station. He picked up Trent Everman again. Boy is looped out of his gourd. Danny wants to know if he should hold him or call his father."

John uttered a curse under his breath, but by the sound of Berta's croaking laughter, she'd heard it. He settled into his cruiser before answering her. "Was he driving?"

"Nope. Walking down Lilac Street, headed toward the bar to see if they'd serve him," she said with a laugh. She and John both knew no one at Pies and Pints would serve anyone underage. The owner, Manny, wasn't a stickler about much, but he didn't serve anyone without legal ID.

"Let him sleep it off in one of the holding cells. No reason to call his dad." That wasn't entirely true. At eighteen, Trent might no longer be a minor, but he was under the legal age for consumption of alcohol. Calling his dad wasn't an option, though.

Not only was calling a parent on an eighteen year old not an option, Trent's dad would beat him senseless for drinking again. John wanted the kid to quit, but not enough to let his dad go after him with his brand of parenting. It was probably that parenting style that had started the kid drinking in the first place. John would figure out another way to handle this situation.

He steered his car out of the hospital parking lot and onto Route 190, heading into the station to see if he could sober Trent up and talk some sense into him. Then he'd come up with a way to get the kid in to see a counselor or to join a support group or something. John sighed. He hated no-win situations, especially ones like this that had him turning his back on something illegal.

When he got there, it was clear Trent wouldn't be in any shape to talk with anyone for several hours—likely more. John left instructions with Danny to call him when the kid was sober and awake then left the station house for the night. Despite telling himself to go straight home, he pulled his patrol car to the side of the road across the street from Alan Bowden's house.

Katelyn's little car was in the driveway and the kitchen and living room lights were on. She'd made it home. John wasn't quite sure what he was doing there. He wanted to know how things had gone with her father at the hospital. He wanted to ask her how she was holding up after seeing her father lying almost unrecognizable in the cold, impersonal hospital room. It had shocked the heck out of John to see the effects of the cirrhosis, the swelling of his face and legs, the discoloration of his skin. He could only imagine what that must have done to Katelyn.

He wanted to comfort her, just as much now as he had when he'd seen her face at the hospital today. His fingers had itched, wanting to reach out and cradle her, hold her tight so her father's words wouldn't cut her so deeply. He'd known, though, she would never accept that from him. Katelyn would never allow him to comfort her.

She'd made it perfectly clear she didn't want to have much to do with him. But they would have to see each other if he was to be any help to her and her father. Which he *would* be, whether she liked it or not.

John scrubbed a hand over his forehead, trying to squeeze out the headache that had settled in behind his eyes. If today had been any indication, dealing with Kate would give him a lot of headaches over the months to come. And yet, here he sat like an idiot, wanting to go inside and make sure she was okay.

John shook his head and forced his gaze off the house as

he threw the car in gear and pulled away from the curb. The last thing he should be doing is sitting in his car wondering how Katelyn was doing and if she would slam the door in his face if he approached.

Probably.

Well, Katelyn could slam all the doors she wanted. Alan needed him now. That was all that mattered.

CHAPTER TWO

The sun shone in through the light, gauzy window curtains of Katelyn's room, stirring her from sleep much earlier than she would have liked. Her eyes felt puffy and swollen, no doubt from the good cry she'd allowed herself the night before. Katelyn wasn't one to cry at the drop of a hat, but seeing her father last night had really thrown her. She knew John had tried to prepare her, but there'd been no preparing for the condition her father was in.

She took in the room around her as she awoke, not used to the pale pink walls of her room in Evers. *Her room.* It wasn't really. She hadn't stayed here longer than one night at a time since she was four years old, and the times she had done that could be counted on one hand. Well, maybe a few more than that, but not many.

The room looked very much the way it had when she was young. The eyelet lace curtains had been changed out for plain white, and the princess border had been removed. The pink walls, rose-colored carpet, and white curtains now made it an acceptable guest room instead of a little girl's room.

She wondered who had made the changes. She doubted it would have occurred to her father to update it. Maybe her Aunt Bea at some point? Katelyn's heart pinched at the thought of her. What she wouldn't give to have her aunt by her side right now, holding her as she'd held her all her life. Bea had been like a mother to her, and Katelyn missed her more than she could ever say.

The nightstand still held the framed picture of Katelyn and her mother, identical to the picture that sat next to her bed in her Austin condo. Katelyn had added a picture of her and her aunt in a frame next to it when she'd unpacked last night. She rolled over and burrowed under the covers, planning to sleep a bit longer, when she heard a not-so-melodious female voice in the house.

"Katelyn, are you up there? Just letting you know it's me down here making noise! I know you artist-types are used to sleeping the day away, but I have errands to run. I can't wait on you all day long, so I'll just start down here."

Katelyn sat up in bed. *Who on earth?* Katelyn fell back in the bed and pulled a pillow firmly over her head. *Mrs. J. must have let herself in.*

This "artist-type" was usually out of bed early, but she'd had a long day yesterday, reorganizing her life in a hurry to get here for her father and escape the fallout of her relationship with Devan. She wanted to burrow deeper into the covers and ignore the noise of Mrs. J. moving through the house, cleaning as she went.

When the vacuum cleaner came on a few minutes later, Katelyn admitted defeat. She crawled from the bed, threw a sweatshirt on over the cami and shorts she was sleeping in and started for the stairs. She didn't dislike Mrs. Jenkins— she just didn't feel like she knew her very well. She'd been Katelyn's babysitter when she was little and now cleaned her father's house. She always acted as if she knew Katelyn so well, but Katelyn had very little memory of her as a child. She'd rarely seen her as an adult, so the familiarity made her a little uneasy.

Katelyn walked into the kitchen to get some breakfast but stopped short at the scene that greeted her on the kitchen counter. Every inch of the counter was covered. There were casseroles, plates of cookies, and more than one barbequed brisket. The vacuum cleaner shut off and she heard Mrs. J.'s voice behind her.

"We'll have to clean out the refrigerator for some of this and put most of it in the freezer. I'll tell people to slow down until you get through a bit of it," Mrs. J. said.

Katelyn turned to face the plump, smiling face of her father's neighbor. "I don't understand. What is all of this?"

"The town's feeding you, of course," Mrs. J. said with a tinge of impatience. Apparently she thought this was something that should be obvious. "Your father's sick, dear. When someone is sick, the town feeds the family for as long as they need."

Katelyn laughed. "That's really sweet, but I don't need anyone to feed me. I'm quite used to feeding myself."

"But you'll be running back and forth to the hospital. And when your father comes home, he'll require a lot of care. This way, you don't have to worry about cooking meals or getting to the grocery store while you're here. You just tell me when you're running low and I'll coordinate restocking things. I come in to clean up once a week for your dad, but if you need more than that while you're in town, just let me know," Mrs. J. said as she started packing casseroles into the freezer.

Katelyn didn't know what to say, so she just smiled and began passing covered dishes over to be stacked with the rest. She couldn't get over the amount of food. Or the thought that she was likely to have a heart attack if she ate the rich casseroles for too long. Everything looked to be covered in cream, butter or gravy. She didn't know why, but the idea of people taking care of her made her squirm.

Mrs. J. talked as they put the food away, not seeming to care very much whether Katelyn answered or not. Actually, she spoke so quickly, it was hard for Katelyn to say much of anything, so she simply didn't. Until it dawned on her that Mrs. J. thought her stay was temporary.

Of course, she would assume that, wouldn't she?

"We'll get your father all settled in back here at home and get you back to your life in Austin. Helen Jensen said she can come to the house a few times a week to check on things. You remember her, dear? Tom Jensen's wife. They own the feed store in town?" She peered at Katelyn over oval-shaped eyeglasses before continuing on. "She took care of her ailing father for years before he passed. Between her and me, we'll stay on top of things, make sure the nurses or whatever are doing their jobs, taking good care of him."

"Oh...I'm not going back," Katelyn said, shaking her head.

Mrs. J. barely looked up from where she was wiping the countertop with a dishtowel. "Well, not right away, of course. I suppose this will be your longest stay in Evers, yet? Hmm?"

Longest yet.

"I'm staying, Mrs. J. I'm not going back to Austin."

Now Mrs. J. looked up, her expression a mixture of shock and disbelief. "But you never stay, dear. And your work is there. Your father told me you need to be in Austin near your gallery." This was accompanied with a nod of her head, as though the topic were finished, the issue decided. This sounded so like her father, Katelyn thought she'd stepped into a creepy episode of *The Twilight Zone* where everyone was able to channel him, despite the fact that he lay in a hospital bed.

"No. I don't need to be near the galleries that represent me. As long as I go for openings and to install any of my larger pieces, I can work anywhere. I'll be looking for studio space in town," she said, drawing a concerned look from Mrs. J.

"But your whole life is in Austin. That's where you live," Mrs. J. said.

Katelyn crossed to the coffeemaker, trying to buy time

19

while she figured out how to handle her extraordinarily insistent neighbor. You would think her father had prepped Mrs. J. on exactly what to say. Either that or Mrs. J. had heard it so often from her father, she could easily mimic his words without any effort or thought.

Katelyn took a sip of coffee and faced Mrs. J. with a smile firmly in place. "Not anymore. I'm selling my condo, well, my aunt's condo really. She left it to me when she passed away. I'm selling it and opening a studio here." This time it was Katelyn who nodded in finality and ended the conversation. She was finished trying to defend her decisions to anyone else.

JOHN STOOD outside Alan's hospital room and watched as Katelyn raised a straw to her father's lips. He couldn't help but admire her emotional strength, even if she was turning out to be a stubborn thorn in his side.

It wasn't easy seeing Alan in this condition. His legs were swollen to the point where he couldn't move them. His face was sallow and his eyes yellow with jaundice. It had to have been a huge shock for her to see him like this. It had been a huge shock to John, and he'd seen the changes happening slowly as the man he thought of as a second father drank himself to death after his "forced" retirement.

Alan had always drank a little more than one might think acceptable, but he kept it under control. He was never drunk on the job, and his officers had always been able to rely on him. But, the drinking got much worse when Alan retired. At that point, John had found him drinking at all times of the day and night. John knew why Alan drank. He had never found his wife's killer. After twenty-four years, the man who'd beaten Caroline Bowden to death in an apparent robbery was still walking free. That was enough to make any man want to disappear in the bottom of a bottle.

Every six months, John and Alan still pored through the scant box of evidence collected at the scene, and John had a feeling Alan looked through the box more often when he was alone. They talked theory and chased any leads that arose, though those were few and far between. Through the years, very little had turned up to point them toward the killer.

As John watched, Alan began talking to Katelyn, but it was quickly clear he was speaking to a ghost, not to his daughter.

"I should have left with her, Caroline. I should have taken Katelyn and run after what she saw, but I couldn't trust anyone else to find your killer. I thought I'd find out who hurt you and bring our baby girl home, but the years went on and the only way to keep her safe was to keep her away. I failed you both, Caroline," Alan said, as he gazed with unfocused eyes at Katelyn.

Katelyn stilled for a split second, then patted her father's hand. John didn't recover nearly as quickly. He was frozen in place as he realized what Alan had said. It took him a minute, but he shook off his surprise and stepped into the room.

"What did Katelyn see, Alan?" he asked quietly, hoping he didn't break the spell Alan seemed to be under, hoping he would say more.

The startled look on his old boss's face told John he wouldn't be getting anything more out of Alan today. "What are you doing here, John? I told you to get on down to the Millers' and take care of that damn dog that keeps getting out. You tell Miller if he can't keep that dog on a chain or behind a fence, I'm gonna have to start fining him."

Alan turned to his daughter. "Mr. Miller's dog gets into Mrs. Cobb's garden and digs up her flowers and she calls us to complain. I've sent deputies out there three times already this week."

John wasn't sure if Alan was seeing Katelyn or still talking to Caroline's ghost. He clearly thought John was still his deputy and he was the current sheriff. In fact, the dog he was talking about had died two years ago. That hadn't stopped the feud between Mr. Miller and Mrs. Cobb. John was pretty sure Miller had buried bones in Mrs. Cobb's garden to teach his new puppy to dig there as well. Either that, or the new puppy was channeling the old dog's ghost. John and his deputies spent as much time as Alan had out there refereeing the two neighbors.

"Alan, a minute ago, you said Katelyn had seen something. Do you remember what she saw?" John tried again.

This time it was Katelyn who cut the questioning off. "Can I speak with you in the hallway, John?"

He ground his teeth together and swallowed a sigh.

With a tight smile at Katelyn, he said his goodbyes to Alan, even though he'd only just arrived.

"I'll stop by again tomorrow." John followed her out to the hallway, but he didn't give her a chance to talk. He knew she'd railroad him if he didn't press her first.

"Kate, has he ever said anything to you like that before?"

John could see her annoyance etched clearly on her face. She was stunning with her long blonde hair and fiery eyes, but she could so easily erase the beauty from her features with one of those pinched looks of hers it was almost amusing. Almost.

"I don't know what he was talking about, John, but you shouldn't be pushing him right now. He needs to rest and stay calm, not get worked up about some nonsense rambling," she said.

"Nonsense rambling? Are you nuts?" John flung his arm toward the room where his mentor lay. "Do you know why he's lying in that bed? Why he drank himself close to death?" John heard her gasp, but didn't stop. She didn't understand what it was like to chase hopeless leads for so many years with no chance of bringing her mother's killer to justice.

"He's had virtually nothing to go on in your mother's case for years, Katelyn. No way to find out who killed her," he spit out. "If there's even a small chance you witnessed something and he's been hiding that all these years, we need to know that. *I* need to know that."

John pushed aside the sick feeling in the pit of his gut at the thought that Alan had lied to him. That Alan hadn't trusted him enough to tell him such a crucial piece of information all these years. He couldn't deal with that right now.

"I didn't see anything. I wasn't there." Katelyn crossed her arms over her chest, a move he was beginning to recognize as her cue she was finished talking to him. Not this time. He wasn't finished. He stepped closer, towering over her with a look that would have sent most of his deputies scattering in the wind. Not Katelyn. She glared back, arms crossed, eyes ablaze.

"You would have been, what? Four years old? You can't be sure you didn't see anything. Maybe this is the reason your father sent you away. Haven't you wondered why he's kept you away?" John knew it was the wrong thing to say the minute he said it, the minute he saw her face.

"I'm sorry, Katelyn. I didn't mean to hurt you," John said, then watched as she transformed the hurt back to anger in a heartbeat.

"Really, John? You think I didn't spend my childhood wanting to know why my father sent me away? You think I need you to solve that little mystery for me? To swoop in and dig and push and get your way no matter the cost to anyone? There are no answers here, John. You can look and poke and prod into my life and his life all you want and it won't lead anywhere. I didn't see anything, John. I wasn't there," she said.

John shook his head. Until now, he might have believed her. He might have bought her denial and walked away. But, what Katelyn had just said gave away a twenty-four-year-old secret. His hands rested on his hips as he leaned down to look her in the eye.

"You see that? What you just did there? You said the exact same thing. 'I didn't see anything. I wasn't there.' You phrased it the exact same way twice. That's what happens when a line is either rehearsed, or it's been fed to you. Did your aunt and father feed you that line so many times when you were little, that now you believe it? Or did you come up with that little lie all by yourself?"

John should have seen the slap coming, but didn't. As with most things revolving around Katelyn Bowden, he was completely caught off guard. It resounded through the hall-ways with stinging sureness. She meant to hit him hard and she did. And before he knew it, she was gone. John rubbed the side of his face as he watched the door to Alan's room swing shut behind her.

He hated to upset her, but Katelyn couldn't possibly understand what was at stake. He finally had a lead in the only unsolved murder in his county; in the one murder his mentor had never been able to solve. John knew if he could just get her to remember what she saw, he could solve her mother's murder before Alan Bowden lost his life. John turned and walked down the hall, feeling hopeful about something for the first time since Alan had been rushed to the hospital four days ago.

CHAPTER THREE

K atelyn walked through the center of town and wondered if she truly could be happy here. In some ways, it was probably foolish for her to move back to Evers now. The doctors said her father didn't have long—six months if they were really lucky, but most likely it would be less than that—and Katelyn really didn't have any other connections in town. Everything was so different than what she was used to in Austin. In Austin, she lived in a small condo right downtown. She could walk to an endless array of restaurants and shops. She could listen to live music or go to shows with friends.

Friends. The same friends who hadn't told her she was dating a married man. The humiliation she'd felt at having fallen for a married man, having been fooled when she should have seen red flags, twisted in her stomach. She should have known there were reasons he never wanted to go out, but Katelyn never really pushed to go out either. She was a homebody. She'd been happy holing up in her condo when they got together. And he hadn't worn a ring or had any tan line from a ring. But, the fact that her friends never told her, never once questioned her actions... Katelyn shook her head. That hurt much worse than the pain of the breakup with Devan. No, she really didn't want to be in Austin right now.

And, for some reason, coming to Evers just seemed like the right thing to do. Maybe some small part of her was hoping her father would beat the odds and live longer than the disheartening prediction from the doctors. If she were really honest with herself, she was probably trying to connect with her father through the town. Maybe after his death she'd find a way to keep him with her by keeping the town in her life.

She walked past T-Bob's Barbeque. Rumor was, Tiny Bob—who naturally was anything but tiny— loved barbeque so much, he'd opened the restaurant just so he could eat barbeque all day. Tiny could usually be found sitting at one of the picnic tables outside the restaurant eating pork ribs or jalapeño sausages and buckets of creamed corn or red potatoes dripping in butter.

On the other side of the street was the post office, followed by a large building that had several functions. The county courthouse that served Evers and many of the surrounding towns as well sat in the center of the building. The fire station connected to one side of the courthouse, while the sheriff's office seemed to grow off the other, as if it had sprung up one day when space was needed rather than being a part of the original building. The rest of that block was filled out with Marshall's Run-On-In convenience store and the First United Methodist Church.

Katelyn lowered her head as she walked past the sheriff's office. She wasn't ready to see John. If she did, she'd need to apologize for that slap the other day and she wasn't ready to offer an apology just yet. Not to mention, one of the nurses had told Katelyn John had already made sure everyone at the hospital knew Katelyn was here and in charge of her father's care. So much for her thinking he was butting in and trying to take over. Truth be told, he'd been nothing but supportive. Even though she hadn't seen him in a few days, she knew he visited her father every day, no matter that he was busy with his duties as sheriff.

After six days in town, word had gotten around that Katelyn was back, and she was greeted with smiles and waves from many people, and curious looks from others. It felt as though some people were happy she was there, while others seemed to want to get a look at the girl whose father didn't want her. She was apparently a legend in this town. Although, there was a thin line between legend and freak show. As she walked through town now, she felt more like a spectacle on parade than anything else.

But, she'd been here almost a week. She needed to find studio space. Katelyn headed past Jensen's Feed Supply where several white-bearded men eyed her with suspicion as they chewed their tobacco on the front steps. She continued down to the end of town that housed several local artists and the Two Sisters Diner. Eight years ago, a well-known painter of landscapes moved to town and opened a studio and gallery that brought some traffic due to the prominence of his name. Another painter followed and opened his studio two doors down. By the time a quilt maker and weaver joined the group, the town had begun to make a name for itself as a spot for a day trip to visit the galleries and studios on Saturday afternoons. Katelyn hoped to find space to put her studio in the same area.

The buildings in this part of downtown were as old as the others, but each had a porch with rocking chairs and hanging plants. It had a charm to it, and she could almost see the gentrification happening before her eyes.

She pressed her nose up against the window of a building that sat across from the diner to see what kind of shape it was in. It was a corner building, with a small side street on one side and the painter's gallery on the other. There was a phone number on the For Lease sign out front, but she wanted to have an idea of what the space was like inside before she called anyone.

"Casing the joint?" came a voice so close to her ear, she could feel the breath on the back of her neck.

Katelyn jumped and spun around to find John Davies' smiling eyes and dimples laughing at her. He reached out to steady her, but the effect of his large, warm hand on her was anything but steadying. Katelyn narrowed her eyes in annoyance at him. And, at herself. Why would she have that kind of response to John, of all people?

And with that, despite all her good intentions of eventually apologizing for slapping him the other day, Katelyn found herself yelling at him once again.

"You scared the wits out of me, John!" she said. "What are you thinking?"

His laugh was deep and rich, and he didn't seem to be holding the least bit of a grudge against her for their argument.

"Sorry. I couldn't resist. You looked like you might try to find an open window any minute there," he said.

Katelyn felt her cheeks flame. She *had* been thinking about looking for an open window.

"Don't worry. Your Uncle Charlie owns the building," John said.

Katelyn hoped he didn't see her flinch at the mention of her 'uncle.' Charlie Hanford was not only the area's biggest commercial property developer, he was also her father's best friend and had, at one time, been her mother's boss. While he seemed like a very nice man, it always felt weird when people referred to him as her uncle. She'd only seen the man on an annual basis, if even that, when she was young. Lately, she hadn't even seen him annually. It had probably been five years since she'd last run into him.

But, before she could object, John was on the phone with Charlie, telling him to come on over and show her the building. She sighed on the inside. She was perfectly capable of calling Charlie and asking him about the building when *she* was ready to see it.

John disconnected the call and grinned at her.

Has he always had dimples?

He was tall, and had a ruggedness to him that was attractive. Oh, let's face it, it was beyond attractive. The man most likely had women swooning over him left and right. Tanned skin and dark eyes, with a smile that would make her want to throw herself at him if he were anyone other than who he was. *Grown men shouldn't be allowed to have dimples.*

And his body. Well, of course, that was honed to perfection with arms that just made a girl want to scream "hold me!" If she were so inclined. Which Katelyn wasn't. Not in the least.

"He and Sam are coming over. I'll wait with you," he said cheerfully as he leaned against the railing and stuck one booted foot on an empty barrel that sat in the corner of the porch.

"Great," Katelyn said, not trying to hide her sarcasm. The man apparently didn't hear it. Either that or he chose to completely ignore it.

"You know Sam Denton, right? He's been your uncle's foreman for years." John took out a stick of chewing gum, popped it in his mouth, pocketing the wrapper. He tilted the pack toward Katelyn, and she took a piece.

Watermelon. Weird choice.

"Yeah, I've met Sam," Katelyn said. She started to turn back to peer through the window, but then spun to face John. "Charlie's not my uncle. You know that, right?"

"Sure. Everyone knows that, but everyone still calls him your uncle, so I guess I never thought anything of it. Does it bother you when people call him that?"

She shrugged. "I just don't know him. It's strange to hear people refer to him as my uncle when I don't really have a relationship with him at all."

John studied her for a second, making Katelyn want to squirm. "Is that why you don't like me? Because you don't know me?"

Geez. Be direct, why don't you?

Katelyn figured it wouldn't hurt to be direct right back.

"Maybe it's because you're controlling, you're bossy, and you're a complete pain in my—"

"Now, now, Katelyn, no need to talk dirty to me," he said with a wink and that damned grin.

Katelyn whirled back toward the window so he wouldn't see the red crawling up her cheeks. His laughter continued to taunt her from behind as she studied what she could see of the inside of the building through the glass.

John didn't say anything for a long time, and when he did speak, Katelyn jumped at the sound. His question was just as out-of-the-blue as his voice had been.

"Kate, don't you think it's possible your dad sent you away because you witnessed your mother's murder?" His voice was quiet, but no less cutting, given the topic.

She didn't answer him. What could she say to a question like that?

"I know you don't want to talk about this, but if we can find out who killed your mother before your dad...well, before he goes, I think we should try. Don't you?"

She turned and looked at John for a full minute before answering. She hoped he wouldn't see that she was trying to compose herself enough to respond. She knew if she opened her mouth to speak just then, she'd probably choke on the sob that seemed to be lodged in her throat at the moment.

"Katelyn?" John prompted again. She shook her head at him and blinked to shove back tears she wouldn't allow to fall in front of him.

"John, I've looked my whole life for a reason for what my father did, but I don't think it exists. You're just grasping at straws. My mom was killed by some petty burglar passing through town, or that construction guy who took off right after she died. Whoever it was is long gone and may very well be dead or in jail now. You need to accept that fact and move on," Katelyn said.

"But—"

"No, stop it! I know you want to think otherwise, but I didn't see anything. I wasn't there." She pressed her lips together, hoping John couldn't see she was close to tears. Mrs. J. was probably right. Maybe she should forget finding a studio here. Maybe going home to Austin was the right thing to do. In Austin, she didn't have to look at any skeletons in the closet or dig up memories that were better left dead and buried. Except in Austin, she was now known as a family-wrecking tramp. *Right. Almost forgot that.*

"Look, I don't mean to be rude, but you don't know me at all. You don't know—" She'd been about to say he didn't know her father, but that wasn't right. He did know her father. He just couldn't possibly understand *her* relationship with her father. She didn't understand it herself. "Just drop it, John, please?"

She heard the quiet plea in her own voice and hated how weak it made her sound.

John stood up, coming close to her, stepping in until his body was only an inch from hers, until she could feel the heat coming off him as they stood toe-to-toe. His face was so close, his eyes looked into hers as if he saw right through her.

She was shocked to find her heart beating rapidly as her breath caught in her throat. Her eyes dropped to John's mouth, which was most definitely not smiling now. Stunned, Katelyn pulled her eyes back up to meet John's gaze and forced herself to breathe.

His voice was soft and low when he finally spoke. "There's that same phrase again. You've been taught to say it, and you don't even know you do it now. 'I didn't see anything. I wasn't there.' You don't even realize you're doing it, do you, Katelyn?"

She opened her mouth but before she could say anything, John stepped back, breaking the hold he'd had over her. They stood watching one another warily, the tension thick and heavy between them. She wanted to deny it, but he was right. She knew if she opened her mouth to deny that she'd seen her mother's murder, the words that came out would be the same words John had just repeated back to her.

How is that possible?

Katelyn looked down at the worn wood of the porch under their feet, forced to wonder if her father had a very good reason for sending her away so many years ago. A reason that had to do with something she saw.

Before she could formulate any response, Charlie and Sam came around the building. The pair looked back and forth between Katelyn and John as though they, too, could feel the weight of the topic that swirled heavily in the air. John was faster than she was. He pasted a smile on his face, offered his hand to first Charlie and then Sam, breaking the spell that surrounded them. With one last strange look in her direction, Charlie unlocked the front door and herded the group into the empty building.

"I was surprised when John called me, Katelyn," Charlie said. "I didn't realize you planned to stay in town."

Katelyn nodded as she looked around at the large interior of the building. She understood why no one expected her to stay. She simply wasn't eager to have the conversation again.

The old house had already been opened up on the inside, and the space was one long room with a few smaller rooms toward the back. She poked her head into a bathroom, closet, and what looked like it was once an office. She couldn't help the flutter of excitement at the idea of opening her own gallery and studio space.

"So, you're moving back permanently then?" Charlie tried again when Katelyn had returned to the group.

"Yes. I've given up my studio in Austin," Katelyn answered, not offering more and hoping he wouldn't push for it.

"Can I see the upstairs?" She needed light for her workspace, and the top floor of the building looked like it would give her just that with all the windows she'd seen from the outside.

"Sure, sure," Charlie said and gestured toward the staircase. "You just, uh, you just take a look and then let me know what you need done to the space. Sam'll get it all fixed up for you."

Katelyn glanced at Sam, but he didn't say anything or indicate he'd heard anything Charlie had said.

She felt John follow her as she started up the stairs.

The top floor had exactly what she needed. Light and space. It would be perfect for her studio, and she wouldn't need to have anything done to it other than a good cleaning and installing some vents. The downstairs would need some remodeling, though.

"Close to Two Sisters," John said, nodding out the front window at the diner that sat catty-corner to the old house. "Good coffee and lots of snacks when you need a break," he said.

Katelyn smiled and nodded, but in reality, she tended to get lost for long periods of time when she was working. She'd forget to eat for hours, if not days, and then need to crash and recuperate. They walked down the stairs quietly, Katelyn's mind whirling with the possibilities of the space.

"How much is the rent, Charlie?"

"'Uncle' Charlie, Katelyn," Charlie said with a smile and a sideways glance at Sam, who still stood mute next to him. "I've got it listed at eight dollars per square foot per year, but if that's too much we can work out a family deal," he said and winked at her.

"Oh, um, great. Thank you. Can I give you a call after I've had a chance to think about it?" Katelyn hadn't been prepared to talk about her studio and what she wanted and negotiate lease terms or anything, particularly in front of a group.

Who am I kidding?

It was John who was making her nervous. She needed to go home and sketch out the space and plot display walls and shipping sections. She wanted time to picture the gallery and the workspace and feel her way around the space in her head. But, more than anything, she wanted to get away from John and have time to think. Katelyn followed the men out of the building with a last long look over her shoulder. A small seed of hope that she'd really found a place to build her future settled into her stomach as they said their goodbyes.

CHAPTER FOUR

At the very last minute, Katelyn chickened out. Never mind all her bluffing about John not being a member of her family. Never mind not wanting him to be part of the conversation she needed to have with her father's doctor. When the time came, Katelyn practically dragged John into the doctor's office alongside her, suddenly terrified at the thought of hearing the doctor's prognosis alone, of facing overwhelming decisions that had to be made with no one by her side to talk them over with.

As the doctor discussed underlying issues that may have sped up her father's liver deterioration and outlined options for making him more comfortable, Katelyn's head spun.

Make him more comfortable?

"You're not doing any treatment?" she asked, feeling like a small child again instead of a grown woman.

John squeezed her hand. "Your father's wishes, Kate. He signed orders refusing treatment of any kind other than measures to ease his pain and suffering." His tone was gentle and kind, but the words made Katelyn crumble.

"But he's not in his right mind, you know that!" Katelyn looked from John to the doctor and back, willing her chin to stop trembling as the words tumbled out. "He's suffering from dementia. How can he make a decision like that?"

John's arms came around her as the doctor explained and Katelyn sank into him. So much for not leaning on John.

"Your father made that decision several years ago," the doctor said, his tone patient. "His lawyer had his Living Will on file and brought it to us when he was checked in. There's no evidence that he was suffering from dementia when he had those papers drawn up, Katelyn. I'm sorry."

When they walked out of the doctor's office half an hour later, Katelyn felt completely wrung out. John took her hand and led her to the hospital cafeteria without a word. And, she followed just as silently. She was numb at the news of her father's condition. John had told her it was bad, but Katelyn felt a little like she'd been hit by a train as John led her to a table and pushed her down into a chair.

He knelt in front of her, those eyes of his on her again, so strong, as if he could will her to be strong with him.

"I'm going to get you something to eat. Stay right here for me, okay?" He said it as though she was a child who might get up and wander away if not supervised, but she just nodded mutely. Information about her father's prognosis and the care he'd need to be comfortable in the coming weeks swam in her head.

"Darlin', can you try to eat something?" John asked, putting a bowl of soup and a corn muffin in front of Katelyn. When she just looked at him, he pulled a chair over and hugged her tight. They stayed like that for a long time, Katelyn soaking in the warmth and strength of his arms, and the feel of his steady breathing as he let her lean on him. He did feel as though he might be strong enough for both of them.

Eventually, Katelyn took a deep breath and pulled back, wiping at tears that had started to fall at some point. She wasn't sure when.

"I don't know whether to do hospice at home or keep him here," she said, referring to the in-hospital hospice program the doctor had talked about. John put a cup of coffee in her hands and wrapped her fingers around the mug.

"You won't be alone if you bring him home—we'll all be there to help you. And we can always bring him back to the hospital if he has symptoms that need to be treated," John said, echoing what the doctor had explained about Alan's care.

When Katelyn didn't answer, John sat back in his chair and changed the subject. "So, did you end up leasing the space we looked at for your studio?"

Katelyn smiled and nodded. She knew what John was trying to do, but she let him. Her heart was still heavy from the overwhelming news the doctor had given her, but it was hard not to feel a bit hopeful at the idea of having a new studio to work in.

"I did. It needs some remodeling to make it work, but I think it will be perfect when Sam finishes the build-out."

"Your dad showed me some of your stuff. It's amazing."

"Thanks," Katelyn said, suddenly feeling shy. She'd always been proud of her work, but her heart flipped a little at the idea that John might really like what she did. She was a sculptor but her work was a little abstract. Not everyone liked it. She worked mostly with metal, but she'd been mixing media lately, dabbling with adding glass and polished stone into her pieces. She'd even started painting a little and then adding texture to the paintings by mixing metals right into the surface of the paints.

"So you'll have a studio and a shop in town?" he asked. Katelyn knew he was trying to take her mind off her father's condition and all the decisions she had to make, but she didn't object. She wanted to think about something other than medical terms and hospice choices, and whether she could really give her father the care he needed in what would likely be his last weeks of life.

She nodded. "I'll have my real studio on the second floor where it's nice and bright. There will be a small work-space downstairs where I'll keep one work-in-progress so people can come in and watch me work or see how a piece progresses. I'll have the gallery in the front and then have the shipping in the back."

"Shipping?"

"Mmm-hmm. I'll still be shipping things back to the gallery that represents me in Austin, and I've got a gallery in New York I ship pieces to, and visit once or twice a year. I also have a gallery in New Orleans that wants to carry a few pieces on a trial basis."

John took a sip of his coffee and pushed the muffin toward Katelyn, encouraging her to eat. She picked at it a bit as he talked. "You know about the painters and potter that opened shops here, I assume? They've brought a real crowd on the weekends during the summer. You should stop in and talk to them."

Katelyn nodded as she swallowed a bite of muffin. "I will. I just want to get settled in a little more before I do," she said, but the truth was, she'd been avoiding people since she came to town.

They sat together in an almost comfortable silence a bit longer. The support John showed her, the incredible help he'd been with her father, the way he'd been almost holding her hand through the whole visit with the doctor—it all served to break down the last bit of resistance to the charm John seemed to exude naturally without any effort at all. Katelyn took a deep breath and spilled the ugly truth she'd been holding onto since she got John's call about her father.

"I've always resented you," she said. "The other day, when you asked me why I don't like you, I lied."

John's eyebrows shot up but he didn't say anything.

"Well, not entirely. You are controlling and opinionated and obnoxiously pushy and bossy." She looked up at him. "You're very bossy."

John began to grin and Katelyn couldn't help but smile back. But her smile was gone in a second as she continued.

"But that's not why I've been, well...the way I've been with you."

"You mean there's more?" he asked, his grin taunting her now.

"I've always resented you for being here with my dad. He wanted *you* here with him. Not me," she said with a little shake of her head as if to shake off the knowledge that she wasn't wanted.

"Oh, Kate—" John began, his smile gone, but she cut him off.

"No, I know it's awful and small and petty of me, and I'm sorry. I've been treating you like dirt, and you've done nothing but help me, help my dad. You really don't deserve to bear the fallout of my twisted relationship with him," she said, her smile wry as she tried to apologize.

John looked at her, seeming to study her for a minute, then scooped up their tray and tossed everything in the trash. He returned and took her hand, pulling her up.

"Come here, I want to show you something." He ignored her protests and pulled her down the hall. They took the elevator up two flights to her father's room.

"Wait here," he said and walked into the room, leaving the door open. With the curtain pulled across the near side of her father's bed, Katelyn could see John and hear her father, but her father couldn't see her standing outside the door.

"John! Hey, boy, how are you? Everything quiet over in Hayes?"

Katelyn cringed. If her father was asking about Hayes,

he was somewhere in the past again. Hayes was the town John had served when he was deputy. Now, as sheriff, he served Evers and ran the rest of the county and its prison system, while one of his deputies had taken over in Hayes.

John played along with Alan's question as if he, too, were still in the past.

"Yes, sir. Everything's all right over there. Hey, how's Katelyn doing, Alan?"

Katelyn listened, stunned as her father's voice came alive. She could hear his excitement, the pride evident.

"Give me my phone, there, on the table," her father said. "She found a gallery that wants to show her work. I always knew she'd make it someday. So much talent. That little girl's got so much talent." John handed her father his phone and she listened as her father showed John picture after picture of what she could only assume were her sculptures. She'd gotten her first gallery showing six years earlier, so she had no idea what pictures her father still had on his phone, but he seemed so excited to be showing John something.

John nodded and caught her eye briefly as she stepped closer to the doorway. Her father missed the look and kept right on going, telling John all about her latest—well, in his mind, her latest—works. Next he told John about the sale of her first commissioned work to the corporate headquarters of a publicly traded company in New York City. Katelyn smiled. She remembered that sale. They'd commissioned a large sculpture for the center of the building's lobby. It had been a huge deal to her at the time. It still was, for that matter.

She listened to her father and John talk as tears ran down her face. Her father seemed to remember every detail of her career, every accomplishment she'd had, and she knew, standing there, this wasn't the first time John had heard these stories. He would laugh and smile with her father and then he'd say something that spurred the next story from her father, as if he, too, had all of her milestones memorized.

For the first time ever, Katelyn let go of the jealousy she'd felt over her father's relationship with John. Instead, she let herself be grateful for it. Grateful that her father had had someone here with him all of these years. Grateful that she had John with her now to help her. Grateful that he'd shown her this—that he'd reminded her of the love her father had for her, despite her unusual upbringing.

A FEW DAYS LATER, Katelyn and John left the hospital together after a morning spent visiting with her father, who had been surprisingly lucid for much of the time. It turned out that getting her feelings out there about her father's relationship with John had been surprisingly...cathartic, actually. Katelyn was able to see John's offers for help for what they were now. Support. Not control.

"So, I've been thinking. You should come out with me and my friends this weekend. We're going to Pies and Pints tomorrow night. It'll be fun: we'll play pool or darts, have a few pitchers and pizza, relax. You can't tell me you don't need to relax," he chided, those dimples eating away at her resistance.

Katelyn squirmed. "I don't think so, John. What if people gawk at me?" She didn't have to tell him why she asked that. He understood she felt self-conscious about her father sending her away. Or rather, the fact that the whole town knew her father had sent her away as a child.

"Don't you read the paper? Watch the news? One of the people going is Laura Kensington. *The* Laura Kensington. As in former wife of Patrick Kensington, chased across the country by the man who killed her husband? *That* Laura Kensington. Well, now she's Laura Bishop because she married Cade Bishop—you remember Cade and Shane Bishop? Cade's the younger one."

Katelyn said yes, but in reality, she didn't remember Cade. They would have been in the same class in school if she'd grown up here and she knew *of* him from her father and aunt, but she didn't actually *know* him.

John continued. "If no one stares at Laura, they're not gonna stare at you. And if they do, she'll know just how you feel and be there for you. Come on. Just one night. Not even a whole night. Stay for an hour. If you're not having fun, we'll fake some emergency and I'll get you out of there."

Katelyn had to laugh. "You sound like a girl planning the 'emergency' text half an hour into a blind date."

John smiled triumphantly. "I promise. Kick me under the table and I'll send a girly text. No one will suspect a thing."

Katelyn smiled back. "Well, at least make sure you slip away to the little girls' room before you send the text so they don't see you."

John laughed. "Perfect. I'll pick you up at six tomorrow."

Katelyn hated herself, because she felt her stomach flip just a little bit at the idea of John picking her up. Like a date. Only not. Because she didn't like John. Well, that wasn't exactly true. She liked him a lot better now that she'd gotten past her resentment and knew him better. But, she didn't like him in *that* way. Only, lately, her body seemed to have other ideas about him.

Yup, just keep telling yourself you don't like this supportive, caring, way-too-gorgeous-for-his-own-good guy with the sexy dimpled smile and the butt you can bounce a quarter off of. Or the shoulders that look broad enough to carry a tank. And, the chest that stretches the limits of his T-shirts in ways that send your imagination running wild. Nope. Not attracted to him.

Yeah, that'll work.

CHAPTER FIVE

Katelyn had to admit, it was a little surreal sitting with Laura Kensington, who seemed a whole lot more down to earth than Katelyn expected her to be. Up close, she realized Laura was just a woman Katelyn's own age who'd been through much more than any woman should have to go through, instead of the socialite everyone was used to seeing on television. And, Laura's friends Ashley, Stacy, and Cora were all just as welcoming and friendly as Laura.

"How's Jamie, Laura?" Cora asked the question as she leaned across the table to scoop another nacho off the plate in between the women. They'd grabbed one of the tall bar tables surrounded by vinyl-covered bar stools near the pool tables. The men were in the middle of a heated game of darts, but it sounded like they were doing more trash-talking than playing. That was all right with Katelyn; it gave her some breathing space from John.

He'd been doting on her since he'd picked her up, but the fact that he was acting so protective and solicitous was only making her cranky. She'd spent so much time resenting John, she didn't know how to handle her body's unappreciated response to him. When he placed a hand on her back protectively or ran his hand up and down her arm softly as they talked to his friends, her traitorous body sat up and took notice. Heck, it practically sat up and begged for more. A little space was a welcome thing right now, until her brain and her body could have a little heart-to-heart about what was and wasn't going to happen with the local sheriff.

She dragged her eyes away from John and the just-right jeans that hugged his hips as he bent over his cue stick. She wanted to wrestle him out of them and see if what was underneath would live up to her imagination, but she forced herself to refocus on Laura.

Laura had pulled out her phone to show them all pictures of her daughter, Jamie, in response to Cora's question. Katelyn grinned. Babies were irresistible.

"How old is she?" she asked as Laura tipped the phone in her direction to show her a round cherub face and blond hair covered in what appeared to be yogurt.

Laura's face glowed as she talked about her daughter. "She's ten months. She turns one in August and she just gets more and more fun each day."

"And more and more spoiled," said John as he came up behind Katelyn, resting a hand on her lower back. He grinned at Cade who came up behind Laura and wrapped his arms around her.

"Guilty as charged," Cade said, not even trying to deny that he spoiled his daughter.

Katelyn could barely focus as John leaned in and whispered in her ear, his breath fanning out to send tingles down her spine.

"Doing okay?" he asked, and she practically had to grit her teeth to keep from yelling at the frustration building in her. She swallowed and nodded, then shifted slightly away from him. She wanted to shift into him instead. Actually, truth be told, she'd like to see how well their bodies would mold together. She wanted to melt into him and find out if his body was really as hard and strong as she imagined it to be.

"I don't think I've ever seen anything like the way that girl has you wrapped around her little pinky," Cora said to Cade with a laugh, drawing Katelyn's focus back to the group. Nothing like talking about a toddler to snap a girl out of a lust-induced haze.

"And all of his other fingers, his toes—you name it, she owns it." Cade's brother, Shane, said as he turned toward Katelyn. "She isn't even a year old and she has her own pony."

As everyone laughed and Katelyn tried to keep her jaw off the floor at the idea of a baby with a pony, Laura came to Cade's defense. "In all fairness," she explained to Katelyn, "he rescues horses at the ranch. It was a natural to keep Millie for Jamie when we saw how gentle she was."

John shook his head and laughed harder, his dark eyes sparkling with true affection that made Katelyn's heart melt just a little. "You can't explain this away, Laura. You know perfectly well he would have gone out and found her a pony if Millie hadn't been there."

Cade shoved at John's shoulder good-naturedly. "She loves it. She squeals every time I put her up on Millie. Besides, I don't actually let go of her or anything. Laura walks Millie and I hang on to Jamie," he said, appealing to Katelyn for approval, but all she could do was laugh at the picture of this big tough guy leading a ten-month-old around on a pony.

Katelyn couldn't stop thinking about John and his hand. It was still on her back. He still stood much too close for comfort. Close enough for her to smell the barely-there scent of a subtle cologne. And, she was still much more distracted by the nearness than she wanted to be. She breathed a sigh of relief when he dropped his hand to pick up his beer.

"So, Katelyn, you seem to be surviving coming home to Evers. You've been away a long time, right?" Cora asked.

Katelyn couldn't tell if she was digging for gossip or not. Her face seemed openly kind, so Katelyn assumed she was genuinely trying to make conversation.

"Yes, I've been in Austin, but I plan to stay here now. I'm leasing space in town for a studio and I'll stay at my dad's for a while, until I figure out where I want to live," she said, trying to think of a way to steer the conversation away from her. She really wasn't any good at that, though. She just drew a blank when she tried to think of new topics.

They must have seen the panic on her face. Ashley

waved a hand dismissively. "Don't worry. We won't grill you about your dad and why you haven't lived at home all these years and where you've been and all that." Cora burst out with an objection and Laura laughed, but Ashley kept right on going, ignoring them. "We're used to being around freak shows. Heck, we are the freak show most of the time."

John's hand had resumed its protective place on Katelyn's back, no doubt to show his support. Ashley continued, "Take Laura. Well, you know all about her. It was all over the news. People still occasionally gawk and stare at her, especially since her wicked ex-mother-in-law moved to town. We just pretend it's not happening when people point and whisper."

Katelyn didn't know what to say, but she was beginning to get the feeling it wasn't unusual for people to be speechless with Ashley. Ashley plowed right on. "My family is another great example. Cora, here, is my sister. Yup, that's right. Sisters who look nothing alike. Our brother, Nathan, is black. So, obviously, again with the 'nothing alike' thing. Sam and Emma are natural siblings, but they're also adopted so our mom and dad aren't really their parents. Not by blood, anyway. So, we're a walking, talking freak show in a town like this."

"I really wish you wouldn't use that phrase, 'freak show.' It's horribly rude. And, we're not freaks. We just have a very eclectic family," Cora said, a small pout on her face.

Laura shook her head at Ashley, still laughing. "You'll get used to our Ash, Katelyn. She tries to keep it all together when she meets new people and she really did a nice job with you for—" she glanced at her watch, "an hour and a half. That's practically a new record. She just can't help it. She has zero filter when it comes to saying whatever crosses her mind, and she makes no effort to word things a little more, um, diplomatically."

Ashley rolled her eyes and shrugged. "I only tell the truth. People just aren't used to it, that's all."

Katelyn laughed, but a small part of her had to admit she liked Ashley's approach to things more than she liked the whispering and stares she'd felt all week. Maybe there *was* something to just speaking your mind.

"I saw your ex-witch-in-law recently, by the way," Ashley went on, talking to Laura. "Came to the library to get a library card, so it appears she plans to stay in town."

This brought a low growl of displeasure from Cade, but Laura brushed it off with a hand to his arm. "I know. She's moved here to try to be closer to Jamie and Justin." Laura turned to Katelyn to explain the pieces of the story Katelyn didn't know. "The quick and dirty version of my past life: you know I was married to Patrick Kensington, right?" Katelyn nodded, even though the question was a bit silly. Everyone knew Laura had been married to Patrick Kensington.

Laura continued. "The witch-in-law is my former mother-in-law, Martha Kensington. Justin is Patrick's brother. He tried to help me last year and ended up getting shot by the man who killed Patrick. Justin lives here now. He hasn't been speaking to his mom since he discovered that she knew Patrick was abusing me and didn't help."

Laura turned back to the group after finishing her rundown. "Apparently, she's been to rehab and is clean now. She wants to try to rebuild the relationships she damaged over the years, or something. I haven't let her see Jamie yet, but Justin told me he's seen her once or twice."

"Mrs. Kensington was apparently too damned drunk the whole time Laura's ex-husband was beating the crap out of her to step in and help Laura," Ashley said, but Laura smiled gently at her.

"I wasn't able to help myself back then, either, Ash. It took a lot to get me to run. Some women never get away."

Cade looked positively reverent as he gazed at his wife. "She and Justin now have a foundation to help women leave abusive relationships. Laura speaks out for women who are feeling as trapped as she was," he said.

"That's amazing that you can put what happened behind you and help other women, Laura," Katelyn said. She didn't know if she would have the courage to share so much of her story the way Laura was doing.

"Oh!" Cora sat up straight with a wide smile on her face. "We should introduce you to Justin. He's great, and single," she finished with a singsong lilt to the end of her sentence, and Katelyn noticed she may have slurred a word or two there at the end. She was a tiny woman so it didn't come as a surprise that a couple of beers might be too much for her.

"No, you shouldn't," came John's deadpan response as the rest of the people at the table hid smiles, and Katelyn tried to hide the blush crawling up her cheeks. John stepped even closer to her, if that was possible.

"Oh no, really, John," Cora said with a swish of an unsteady hand in John's direction. "Really. I promise. Justin's fine. He's not at all like Laura's husband was. He's the sweetest guy," she said with a sly smile at Katelyn. "And sooooooo gorgeous," she stage whispered as Katelyn's eyebrows went up and everyone gave up on their attempts to stop laughing. John glared, Katelyn burned bright red, and Cora looked around in confusion.

"Well, he is gorgeous." She looked to her sister for help. "You said so yourself, Ashley. A butt like a Greek god, remember?"

Ashley shook her head at her sister. "I'll explain later, sweet girl."

The chatter resumed for a few minutes but was interrupted again by Cora's sudden realization. "Oh!" She looked back and forth between John and Katelyn. "Oh," she said again, drawing the single syllable out.

"And, that's our cue to go. Night, everyone!" Ashley said as she slid from her seat and pulled Cora from her chair. She gathered their purses and started to herd Cora toward the front door. "I'm really glad you came out with us, Kit Kat," she called out over her shoulder.

Katelyn didn't have a chance to be dismayed at Ashley's apparent choice of a nickname for her. She was too busy trying to talk her fluttering heart down out of the clouds. So what if John had just acted as if there was something between them? So what if he almost acted as though they were together—or at least acted as though he wanted them to be together. The fact that he told Cora in no uncertain terms that setting Katelyn up with another man was off limits shouldn't have sent her heart into a stuttering, stumbling mess. But it did.

KATELYN HADN'T STOPPED THINKING about the previous night out with John all day, and it was beginning to irritate the daylights out of her. The whole ride home, she'd fantasized about what it would be like to be on a date with John. Which was ridiculous since John Davies was the last man she'd want to be on a date with. She didn't like him. She resented him. She wanted him to buzz off and leave her alone.

Oh, who was she kidding? Those feelings were long gone. Somehow, in his steadfast support for her in the middle of all that was going on with her father, he'd wheedled his way in. She was flat-out, dead-on attracted to the man. She didn't know if it was the dimples or the muscles... oh, the muscles. God, what that man did to a shirt when it stretched out over his chest and hugged his arms with just the right amount of tautness to set her eyes wandering along hard lines and a well-cut six-pack.

So annoying.

Katelyn focused on putting one foot in front of the other as she pushed herself on a five-mile run. It was meant to take her mind off John, but it wasn't having the desired effect at all. She'd thought of nothing but the way he'd grazed his hand over her back or whispered in her ear last night. Of the way he'd looked for a split second when he'd walked her up to the door last night, as though he might kiss her goodnight. As though he would close the inches between their mouths and press his lips to hers. Those lips that made her want to lean in and nip at them just to see what he'd do. To see if she could break that cool, collected facade he always had going.

She'd held her breath, not knowing if she wanted him to kiss her or to stop, and somehow wanting both things at once.

He hadn't kissed her. He'd said goodnight and walked away, making her wonder if she'd imagined things.

Katelyn pulled herself out of her thoughts and realized she'd seriously miscalculated her run. It had gotten darker much earlier than she thought it would. Either that or she'd been out a lot longer than she'd realized. As she jogged along the old dirt road that would bring her back to her father's house in another half mile, Katelyn frowned. It was dark and getting darker by the minute, with no street lights.

It hadn't even occurred to her that there weren't street lamps on most roads out here. The houses were much further apart and set back from the road once you got outside of town, so porch lights were no help either. She picked up her speed realizing she couldn't be seen easily if a car passed by. She was wearing a gray shirt and black running pants and she hadn't worn her reflective vest.

She immediately went to thoughts of John coming to

her rescue, and she actually rolled her eyes and fought the urge to slap herself silly. Just because she was running after dark on an old dirt road didn't mean she needed John to come and save her. And even if he did save her, that didn't mean it would end in her kissing him senseless at the relief of being safe. And, even if she *did* kiss him, she had to wonder now if he would kiss her back. Why hadn't he kissed her last night? Maybe all the touching last night had just been his way of being supportive? But then why freak when Cora mentioned setting Katelyn up with Justin? Katelyn groaned in frustration.

Forget him! She knew she had a tendency to over-analyze things, but this was plain ridiculous.

Headlights cut through the dark coming toward Katelyn, and she raised her arm to protect her eyes from the glare at the same time that she went further onto the shoulder in case the driver couldn't see her. Nerves danced through her body, as what looked like a truck seemed to slow for a minute. She wondered if the driver was going to offer her a ride. Evers might be a small town and most of its residents wouldn't hesitate to take a ride from one another, but Katelyn knew all too well what could happen even in this small town haven. Her mother had lost her life in a very violent way in this town and Katelyn wasn't about to forget that.

Before she realized what was happening, the truck sped up and was heading directly at her. Katelyn shifted slightly to the side, but the truck seemed to shift with her. She'd like to say she reacted swiftly and calmly and moved out of the way, but that wouldn't be true. In fact, she wasn't calm or rational or anything of the sort. She was confused. Her brain couldn't process the truck coming at her, so it simply didn't. Rather than fathom that it might hit her, she kept telling herself the truck wasn't going to hit her. It was a prank. The driver would swerve at the last minute.

But it didn't. Katelyn dove out of the way as the truck roared by, bearing down on her. Pain shot through her left knee and burned up the side of her arm from wrist to shoulder. She lay face down in a shallow ditch by the side of the road listening in shock to the sound of the truck's engine as it faded away. She knew before she even moved that the walk—or rather limp—home would be long, sore, and filled with pain.

Yup. She couldn't see the road rash up the left side of her body, but she could tell it was there. She could feel blood trickling down her arm and her knee felt like a basketball. Katelyn reached into her pocket for her phone before she realized she didn't have anyone to call. She wasn't close enough to anyone in Evers to have their phone numbers. Well, she had John's number, but if she called him, he'd make a big deal out of this. That wasn't at all what she needed right now. Not to mention, she was a little embarrassed by the whole thing. She should have just moved further off the road to begin with. She should have seen what was about to happen and reacted faster. No. She wanted to forget whatever idiot had just chased her off the road and get into a hot bath.

Limping home at a pace that could be outdone by the

slowest snail on the planet won out over calling John. Twenty minutes later, she let herself into the house and slipped into a bath, wincing as the hot water surrounded her. She didn't make it into bed for another few hours. Instead, she became intimately cozy with the tweezers in her father's first-aid kit as she pulled bits of rock and sand out of her arm and leg and iced her knee.

When she finally did crawl into bed, she had to lie on her right side and prop pillows around herself to keep from rolling during the night. Her whole left side felt like it had been shaved down with a cheese grater. But there was one good thing about the whole ridiculous episode: it definitely helped keep her mind off John Davies and the almost-kissing-episode.

CHAPTER SIX

"Hey, John," Deputy Danny Widen said as he knocked on the door and poked his head in John's office. "I'm taking off for lunch."

"Mmm." John nodded absently but kept his eyes on the evidence and coroner's report spread out on the table in front of him. After the way he'd felt last night with Katelyn —as though he wanted to tear her clothes off, rip any man who looked at her to shreds, and take her right there in the bar to claim her as his—well, he needed to focus on putting her back in the category she belonged in. He didn't have a clue why he'd acted like he had when he and Katelyn had gone out with his friends. One minute, she was irritating the daylights out of him with her prickly attitude and stubborn pride and the next, he'd been fantasizing about her on a pool table.

Katelyn was his mentor's only daughter and a woman who had made it clear she didn't like him. To top it off, he was fairly sure she'd seen something when she was little. She was potentially a witness to the only major crime this tiny town had ever seen: her mother's murder, which meant he had no business going near her in anything other than a professional way.

Years before, during his undercover stint in New York City, he'd gotten involved with a witness. It ended with Lexi dead and him wishing he were too. He'd come to Evers, running from ghosts and a past he couldn't bear to face. It had been Katelyn's father who slowly pulled him back from the anger and hatred he was drowning in. He wouldn't repay Alan by sleeping with his daughter or putting her in danger by losing focus like he had in New York.

Ha! As if she'd ever want that to happen. He hadn't been able to keep from touching her last night at every opportunity, but she'd moved away any chance she could. The woman had made it clear she wasn't interested. Why couldn't he just leave it at that and walk away?

Danny's voice cut into John's thoughts again. "Heard you took Katelyn Bowden out the other night."

There was a grin in Danny's voice that told him the whole office was probably talking about John and Katelyn. John raised his eyes to give him a look sure to cut off that topic before it began.

Danny cleared his throat and raised his hands in surrender. "Sorry. Never mind."

John sighed. "It's all right, Danny. Have a good lunch." He shouldn't be biting the heads off his guys just because it was obvious to everyone around him that he had a thing for Katelyn.

"What's that?" Danny asked, stepping further into the room and eyeing the contents of the table. John usually worked on Caroline Bowden's case at home or at Alan's house. The young deputy in front of him probably didn't know anything other than what the newspapers had printed or the rumor mill had churned up over the years. John had pulled out the case files and grabbed the evidence out of storage today to remind himself that Katelyn was a witness. She was a link in the case and nothing more to him. It wasn't working, but at least he could tell himself he was trying.

"Caroline Bowden's case file," John said, looking up at Danny. "I keep hoping I'll see something new since Alan, well, you know..." John didn't mention his theory that Katelyn had seen the murder. The less anyone knew about that, the better.

"I've never seen the file," Danny said, and John couldn't miss the hopeful tone. Danny was young and eager. He didn't have any experience working a case like this, but it wouldn't hurt to have someone new look at it. And, maybe in explaining things to Danny, John might make a connection or see something he'd missed all these years.

"Fresh eyes can't hurt," John said, sliding some of the papers toward Danny.

Berta poked her head in the room. "I've got fresh eyes. Well, that's not true. They're old as dirt. But they're fresh on this," she said with a nod toward the table.

John waved her in.

"There isn't much to the file. Caroline Bowden was found by her employer, Charlie Hanford." John didn't have to tell Danny or Berta who Charlie Hanford was. Everyone in town knew Charlie as the owner of the biggest real estate development company in the area. He'd been responsible for building the large retirement community, Sol City, just outside of town back in the 1980s, and still owned most of the commercial real estate in town.

John picked up the file and read off the pertinent details. "She was murdered on February 27, 1986 in an apparent robbery. Caroline was Charlie's bookkeeper and she routinely worked out at his house in the home office he keeps there, since his job site offices move around from site to site as he works on different projects. Charlie kept petty cash of about $2,000 in a small lockbox in his desk. The lockbox and money were missing. Caroline had been beaten to death. Charlie found her and called it in, but she couldn't be revived. She was dead when the paramedics arrived."

"Murder weapon?" Danny asked, pointing to the sealed evidence bag that contained a heavy stone bookend. It was a carved statue of some kind of ancient deity with a squat round body and three arms extending out on either side. It was ugly as sin but quite distinctive.

"No." John shook his head. "We never found the murder weapon, but this is one-half of a set Charlie had on the shelf near his desk. The other is missing. Caroline was found right next to his desk. There's a door leading from the office out to a patio and the backyard. That lock had been broken from the outside."

John picked up the stone bookend in its plastic evidence bag. "The coroner said this matched the wounds on her head, so we believe the matching one was the murder weapon. The assailant likely took it with him when he fled the scene. We kept an eye on pawn shops in the area and put out a notice about it to shops all around the state. It's a fairly valuable piece according to Charlie, so we hoped we might catch a break when the murderer tried to sell it, but it's never turned up."

Danny picked up the notes from the responding officers on the scene. They had both retired years ago and one had passed away a few years back. Alan Bowden was on scene, of course, but didn't work the case. He'd written his own notes that weren't part of the official file, but Danny scanned those next, as well as the coroner's report before handing them to Berta to read. John waited patiently, wondering if anything might jump out.

"Not much here," Danny said dejectedly, as he set the papers down and looked at the table. He was right. There had been no foreign prints and many of the surfaces, including the drawer where the petty cash was kept, had been wiped clean. There were no witnesses. The woman who cleaned Charlie's house hadn't been there that day and Charlie had seen nothing suspicious when he arrived home. There was, in fact, nothing to go on.

"The theory has always been it was that guy who worked for Charlie, right? What was his name?" Danny asked, and John could see he wanted to come up with an answer as much as John did. There just weren't any answers. He needed to see if he could jog Katelyn's memories. Help her remember what, if anything, she'd seen as a child.

"Ken Statler. The guy had only worked for Charlie for a month before the murder and he disappeared right after. Everyone thought he needed money, knew about the petty cash, and went there to steal it. Theory is, when Caroline walked in on him, he killed her and then took off. He was never spotted again after that."

Danny looked at John almost apologetically. "It's a sound theory."

"Except when you take into account that Ken Statler drove a nice truck and had a great set of tools he took with him from job to job," Berta said. "My sister's husband worked with him some. Said he was a real standup guy. He was known to work for a contractor for a short time before moving on, but he had worked his way through this part of Texas a couple times over the years. Never heard a bad word about that guy. Why would he need to steal if he had that truck and all those tools?"

John shook his head. He hadn't been in town when the murder happened, so he could only go by what was in the reports. "None of his past employers ever had a bad word to say about the guy, except that they wished he would have stuck around longer. He just didn't seem to like to stay in one place, but that's no crime. And, you're right. With a truck and tools like that, if he needed money, he could have sold either of those instead of turning to burglary and assault."

Danny grunted his agreement and picked up one of the sets of notes he'd looked through earlier. "Yeah, but his truck was seen in Charlie's driveway. Red pickup. Late model Ford."

A half grunt came from Berta.

"What?" John asked and watched his dispatcher intently.

She looked at the younger men with exasperation clear on her craggy features. "Half a dozen men around town drove a red truck back then. Heck, I could probably walk outside and find five or six late model Ford pickups on this block that are red." She started ticking off names on her fingers. "Don Canton, Big Earl Walters, his son Little Earl, Sam Denton.... They all had one back then."

"Sam?" John asked as he held his breath, a hard knot forming in his gut.

She nodded. "Sure. Sam Denton had a red truck up until ten, twelve years ago. And he used to be parked up at Hanford's place all the time for work—still does. And Little Earl went by there sometimes to drop stuff off for his dad. His daddy owns that office supply place out on Route 190. Little Earl made deliveries. So, he'd be up at Charlie's place sometimes, too. Who's to say if Ken Statler was really there that day if no one saw him or at least a license plate or something?" They'd all read the notes. They knew the witnesses hadn't specified. They'd just said a red truck.

All three of them stood and stared at the evidence on

the table, as if they hoped something would jump up and wave at them, leading them to the right answer. Instead, it seemed they'd succeeded in making things murkier than they'd ever been.

"Danny, can you see if Marcy Whorton still lives in town? She was the neighbor who reported the truck. See if she actually remembers seeing Ken Statler there or if she just assumed the truck was his."

"Marcy moved out to Sol City years ago. I'll try to find out if she's still there," Berta said as she left the room.

John got up and clapped Danny on the shoulder. "Go get some lunch then touch base with Berta about Marcy Whorton. If she's still at Sol City, get out there in the next day or so and talk to her."

"You got it, boss," Danny said as he left.

And I'll figure out how to get Katelyn to remember what she saw, what her father and aunt tried to protect her from all these years.

John couldn't imagine why Alan had never told him about Katelyn. Maybe Katelyn told her father what she saw when she was a child—before she blocked it out. Maybe Alan had already chased that lead and dismissed it. John had to admit, though, the fact that Alan apparently hadn't trusted him with that secret ate at him. He stared back at the evidence on the table and wondered how much more Alan hadn't told him.

∼

John stepped out through the double doors of the hospital's north entrance into the blinding heat of the Texas sun. He didn't really mind the heat most days and definitely preferred it to cold, but his uniform wasn't exactly made for staying cool and comfortable. He resisted the temptation to undo several buttons of his shirt. He might just have to talk to the uniform rep who kept coming by the office with samples of special wicking fabrics and uniform shirts that were vented along the sides and back for hot weather.

The way this summer was heating up, he might even let the rep convince him that wearing shorts as part of his force's uniform wasn't completely unprofessional looking.

The trip to the hospital hadn't gotten him any closer to figuring out what, if anything, Katelyn might have witnessed. Alan had been asleep when he arrived, and he was groggy from the pain medication they were giving him. The nurse told him they'd had to increase the dosage to try to help him get some rest through the pain.

John looked out toward the parking lot, planning to head left toward his cruiser, but a flash of blond caught his eye instead, making him swing right. *Katelyn.*

What the heck? She was limping and moving slower than Berta trying to avoid a direct order.

"Katelyn!" he called out as he jogged toward her. "What happened?" He took her small hand in his, turning her arm over gently to reveal a huge swath of livid road rash up her left side. The sight of it made him sick. He wanted nothing more than to pull her into his arms and hold her. Something he knew for sure she would hate. Not to

71

mention something he shouldn't be doing. He needed distance between them, and holding her sure as hell wouldn't put it there.

She pulled her hand back slowly, almost as if to prove his point, as if she'd read his thoughts. "Nothing. It's not a big deal. I fell last night when I was out running."

John wondered if she pulled back out of embarrassment or pain or something else.

"You fell?" he echoed. John looked at Katelyn and waited for a better explanation. You didn't get road rash like that from tripping and falling.

She shook her head at him as if he were a child and she had all the patience in the world for his pitiful inquiries. "You can stop worrying, John. It really was nothing. I went out running and forgot there aren't any lights at night here. It got darker much faster than I thought it would and I wasn't wearing a reflective vest. A truck came at me and I had to jump out of the way. End of story."

"You could've been killed. What were you thinking? And why didn't you report it?" he asked, and although he knew he was towering over her and intimidating her, she didn't back down, didn't flinch a bit. Damn. He wanted her to flinch. To take this seriously. To worry just a little bit about the gravity of the situation. About the real possibility she could have been killed.

The thought that she could have been hurt out there bothered him a hell of a lot more than he'd like it to. The least she could do was take his concern seriously.

She brushed it off like it was nothing. "I get it. It was

bad. But it was probably just teenagers messing around and they took it one step too far. I just don't want to make a big deal out of it, okay?"

"Katelyn, if there are kids out playing chicken on my roads, I need to know about it. You had no way of knowing if they were drinking, or if they'd try that with someone else who couldn't get out of the way in time. It wasn't your call to make. You should have called me."

Her sigh didn't go unnoticed. "You're right. Slap me on the wrist and send me on my way," she said, holding out her good wrist for him and sending all kinds of images into his head. She probably hadn't had any intention of putting those images in his head with her little reference to punishment, but there they were. His head was flooded with thoughts he couldn't really handle right at the moment. Not standing here in broad daylight where anyone could see the effect those thoughts would have on his body any minute, if he wasn't careful.

John took a step backward and nodded.

"You're right. Sorry." He looked over to his cruiser. "I have to get going. I just stopped by to see your dad, but I have to get back to the station." *And put some distance between us. A lot of distance.*

Katelyn smiled and said goodbye. It wasn't until John was pulling out of the parking lot that he began to have a nagging little thought at the back of his mind. He wondered, just for a brief second, if the incident with the truck had really been kids messing around. If it was possible that John wasn't the only one who suspected Katelyn had seen more than she realized—more than anyone realized—when she was a little girl.

John shook his head and ignored his paranoid delusions. What happened to Katelyn was nothing more than a prank. Nothing more.

It took Katelyn a lot longer than it should have to get to her father's room. Everyone she encountered along the way wanted to know what had happened, why she was limping and sore. The nurses at the front entrance, the candy striper who helped deliver the meals to her father's room, and finally, the nurses at the station down the hall from his room. For them, she shortcut the story to, "I tripped and fell," and hurried past them into the room.

Her father, on the other hand, didn't notice her injuries. He was agitated and angry today, wanting to know why she wouldn't let him go home. He seemed to be seeing her as her mother again, although she couldn't be entirely sure.

And, Katelyn herself wasn't feeling all that patient and calm. No matter where she went, she ran into John. When he took her hand in his today and looked at her injuries with such care, he'd damn near taken her breath away. *Jerk.*

She didn't want him taking her breath away if he wasn't going to act on it. Which, apparently, he wasn't. Katelyn winced. She was really off her game when it came to reading men. Broken man radar, she thought. It sure wasn't working when she dated Devan and it still wasn't working now. Seeing John left her edgy and annoyed.

It hadn't helped that she'd caught the scent of pine cleaner on her way in today. The smallest whiff of pine could send Katelyn's head reeling, whipping her into a nightmarish memory she knew only existed in her mind. She had no idea why the scent of pine brought forth the false memory of her mother's scream, but she forced it out of her head and gritted her teeth against nightmares she knew weren't real.

Her father's voice drew her out of her thoughts.

"I want you to talk to the doctors. They're keeping me here when there's nothing wrong with me." Katelyn didn't point out the jaundice, or the way his abdomen was swollen and distended from the fluid pooling in it as a result of the liver disease. Pointing things like that out just served to pull him out of his dementia too harshly. The resulting jolt would cause him such distress, she'd rather let him rail at her than give him a reality check that would break his heart.

"I'll talk to them today, Dad," she said softly, swallowing the sigh that threatened as she thought about having another talk with the doctors. She had spent the morning on the phone with a nursing company discussing options for in-home care, and then surfed the Internet to find somewhere to rent the hospital bed and monitors she'd need to bring him home.

Her answer somehow just ramped him up even more and he began to yell about conspiracies to rob his insurance company blind. "Just because I have a good pension and health insurance, they think it's okay to bilk the insurance company for every procedure they can think up. They'll take everything if you give them an inch, Katelyn."

Well, that was good. At least he saw her standing next to his bed instead of her mother this time.

"Hey, Alan, thought I'd swing by for a game of cards. Hi, Katelyn," said Charlie as he walked in the door, pulling a deck of cards from his chest pocket. Seeing how patient and easy Charlie was with her father made Katelyn grateful for the friendship that had stood the test of so many years. Having Charlie here to help through such a debilitating disease was a blessing to Katelyn and her father.

Charlie could usually snap her father out of his foul moods and he seemed to have patience when hers was wearing thin. Her father was taking more out of her than she'd like to admit as she tried to come up with a way to get him the care he needed from home instead of the hospital.

"Charlie!" her father said, and suddenly became the jovial friend everyone in town remembered him as. Charlie and her father had been best friends for as long as Katelyn could remember. She kissed her father goodbye and slipped out the door, feeling guilty for leaving so quickly, as Charlie pulled a chair up to the side of the bed and shuffled the deck. Charlie winked at her as she looked back, but her father was already picking up his cards and talking baseball with his friend. Katelyn gave a relieved smile and a small wave of thanks to Charlie then took her sore body back home to bed.

CHAPTER SEVEN

It was about a week before Katelyn could walk without limping. Running during that time had been out of the question. It seemed the skin down the left side of her body was going to take a lot longer to heal. It felt stiff and tight whenever she moved, not to mention the itching as the scrapes scabbed over. Still, by the following week, she felt a lot better. She began to get out for shorter runs again, always being sure to wear a vest with reflective patches now and sticking more to the main roads.

The doctor still hadn't cleared her father for home care, even though Katelyn had planned out the nursing care and equipment she'd need. Alan needed to have the liquid drained from his abdomen routinely now and they felt if she took him home, she'd only be back with him in a day or less.

She'd met Ashley and Cora for lunch at Tiny-Bob's earlier in the day. They'd been right. The pork ribs melted in your mouth and the brisket was better than anything she'd tasted in Austin, which was hard to believe given how many award-winning barbeque spots they had there. Katelyn knew she'd turned bright red when Ashley asked her how John was, but they'd all laughed over her response. They laughed even harder at Cora's response when Ashley asked about Justin.

Apparently, despite Cora's talk about setting Katelyn up with Justin the other night, she was really the one who wanted to be set up with him. Katelyn was tempted to ask her why she didn't go for it if she liked him, but didn't feel she knew Cora well enough yet. Besides, with Ashley for a sister, Cora was probably getting enough pressure as it was.

Katelyn looked around at the progress being made in her studio space and smiled. Her life in Austin might have imploded, her father's health was swiftly declining, but *this,* at least, was going right. Her fingers tingled with the urge to get back to her art, but the build-out had to be done before she could set up the studio. Seeing the progress Charlie's foreman, Sam, and his crew were making, made Katelyn feel hopeful at the end of what had been a very long day of talking to doctors and listening to her father ask about going home.

It was late by the time she left the hospital, but she had stopped by the studio anyway. Charlie had given her a key even though she hadn't technically taken possession yet. It was quiet and still at night, but she could picture what it would be like when she opened. She could see her pieces displayed throughout the gallery. Her sculptures in the center and her newer paintings mounted on the walls.

She smiled as she ran her hand over the half wall that would separate her downstairs work space from the gallery. It would be hard to get used to having people watch her work, but she had talked to several artists who'd done this type of open-studio concept and the results had been great. Besides, she'd have her full studio upstairs and that would be closed to the public. Many artists felt an open studio brought more foot traffic in the door, and people seemed more likely to buy after feeling they had a connection to the artist.

Things were coming together. With a final look around the room, Katelyn flicked off the work light and let herself out the back door. As she turned back to slip the key in the lock, a shadow crossed behind her and her thoughts went to John, happy he had stopped by to check on her. She couldn't help the smile that spread across her face. Her belly filled with butterflies at the thought of his smile, those dimples.

Even if they only had a few minutes before he had to get back to work, she'd take it. The man made her stomach do flip flops when he ran a hand casually down her arm or stood just that tiny bit closer than necessary. And, whenever she saw the heat in his eyes as his gaze raked over her, tingles lit up her body. When that happened, she imagined what it would feel like to have his hands join his eyes in their exploration. What would it feel like if his mouth joined his hands?

As Katelyn turned, eager to see John, her smile quickly dropped. Someone shoved her from behind. This wasn't

John. This was all wrong. She cried out in pain and shock as her body hit the door she'd just closed. She fought for some semblance of balance but all she found was confusion, panic and pain.

"Time to leave, Katelyn. You don't belong here," a voice growled in her ear. The person shoved her harder against the door, slamming her head into the cold metal. She raised her arms to block the blow but they were useless against the strength behind her. Her head hit metal. She heard and felt the resounding crack. The sound alone would have sickened her but the sharp bolt of pain to her skull brought its own nausea. Bile flushed her throat.

She couldn't see who was pinning her to the door. A hood was pulled down over his face. He pressed his arm into the back of her neck to prevent her from turning to look at him. She opened her mouth, but no sound escaped. Her mind raced. She tried to control the panic setting in, but the situation quickly overwhelmed her.

She shut her eyes and tried to stop the sob that wracked her body, but couldn't. Fear gripped her, building deep in her belly, her heart racing as her throat constricted. She smelled the man's breath, foul and laden with alcohol. He reeked of strong body odor as though he hadn't washed in days. The realization that she was so completely at his mercy hit her hard. She opened her mouth wider to scream, but before she could, he gripped the back of her hair and slammed her head into the door. Once. Twice. Again and again. She began to pray. For him to stop. For her to be spared the pain. That he wouldn't rape her. Kill her.

Katelyn held on as long as she could, trying to raise a scream, to call for help. Then blackness swallowed her as she felt herself fall.

JOHN TURNED his cruiser onto Lilac Street and drove through the dark quiet of Evers. He'd take one pass before dragging himself home for the night. It had been a long day. He'd had to go to the county prison for what turned into a three-hour meeting, and then over to the opposite edge of his county to help out on a prisoner transport because half his deputies were out with the flu. With his luck, he'd catch the flu and bring it back to the rest of his men.

The town seemed to be locked up tight as he looped behind the businesses to cut through the alley on his way home. They didn't have much crime in Evers, but John always thought having a police force that was embedded in the community was one of the reasons for that. He liked to tuck the town in at night when he could.

He neared the galleries and his thoughts switched to Katelyn—not unheard of nowadays, since she was on his mind at least ninety percent of his waking hours. Shoot, she was on his mind a hell of a lot of his sleeping ones, as well. He wondered how her studio was coming along. A glance at the clock told him she was probably at home already, maybe getting ready for bed. His thoughts ran to images of Katelyn slipping out of her clothes for bed and he groaned, shifting in his seat. He really had to stop torturing himself like that.

John's headlights swept over a crumpled form at the back of Katelyn's studio. They didn't have a big homeless population in Evers, but there were a few guys who might have a little too much to drink and end up passing out on the steps of one of the businesses instead of making it home. John aimed his spotlight toward the figure and threw the car in park. With any luck, he could rouse the person and figure out who he needed to call to help them home. Then, he'd get home and hit the shower before crawling between the sheets for a few hours of sleep before his next shift.

Two more steps and he saw Katelyn's blond hair splayed out on the pavement. His stomach pitched wildly as he ran to her, a vicious curse on his lips.

"Kate!" John knelt next to her, his eyes going to the blood seeping into her hair from a wound on her temple. "Talk to me, Kate," he said, praying for once she'd listen to him. Or sit up and argue with him. He'd take that, too.

Her eyes fluttered and she mumbled something. John squeezed her hands, probably harder than he should have, but he needed her to wake up. He radioed for an ambulance and tried to get her talking. But all the while he could feel the rage building in him.

This wasn't a fall. The amount of blood, the tear in her shirt at the neckline. Someone had done this to her. Someone had hurt her on purpose.

John schooled his voice, ensuring that his anger wouldn't come through. "Hang on, honey, the ambulance will be here in a minute. Can you talk to me? Do you know where you are?"

"John?" she said. Her eyes grew a bit panicky. He held her down gently, one hand on either shoulder.

"Shhh, honey. Don't try to sit up. We'll wait here together. Do you remember what happened?" The look of fear in her eyes told him she was reliving it right in front of him. He heard the ambulance coming and focused on looking her in the eye. Keeping her talking, as calmly as he could. His mind raced as he tried to think of something to ask her that wouldn't make her even more fearful.

"I'm here, and I'll stay with you. Tell me what day it is, can you remember?" *Idiot. That's all you can come up with?* All his training and experience in handling a crisis seemed to have flown the coop.

"Friday," she answered, and John smiled as the EMTs came up behind him. He shifted to let them in with a backboard, but didn't drop her hand.

"That's right, honey. Friday. You had lunch with the girls today, right? What wild things did Ashley have to say today? Anything good?"

He kept right on with the ridiculous conversation through the whole ambulance ride. He even laughed when Katelyn told him Ashley had talked about his butt at lunch and filled her in on all of his ex-girlfriends in town. *Great.*

John knew when they got to the hospital he'd have to take her statement to find out who had attacked her, but for now, he just wanted to keep her calm until they could get her to a doctor. He didn't think his heart had ever had the kind of scare it had when he'd seen that blood staining her hair red like that. John took a steadying breath as the ambulance pulled into the emergency bay. He needed to switch back into law enforcement mode, make the change to someone who would collect evidence, bag her clothing, question the victim, and find her attacker. But, damn, having Katelyn as the victim made that hard.

"LEAN ON ME, SWEETHEART." John said, wrapping his arm around her middle and pulling her close, as he walked her up the front steps of her father's house. He had been nothing but sweet, and gentle, and solicitous since he found her unconscious outside her studio door.

He had stayed with her every minute at the hospital, and she'd seen him almost come out of his chair when the doctor asked if she'd been raped. She was weak with relief that she hadn't been, but she'd never forget the fear of thinking it was possible as her attacker's hands slammed her into the wall.

John told the doctor he'd spend the night with her, waking her every two hours to check for signs of concussion. And Katelyn had let him promise with no argument. She didn't want to be alone right now. She had no idea what had happened, what the man who attacked her had meant when he'd told her it was time to leave town. For now, all she wanted to do was sink into John's strong arms and imagine she was safe again.

"Thanks," she murmured as he helped her down onto the couch. She'd already told him everything she could remember about the attack while they were at the hospital. She hadn't seen the man who attacked her, hadn't been able to identify him from his voice, which sounded like he had been masking it anyway. She doubted he really spoke in the gravelly voice he'd used to warn her off.

"Wait right here. I'll get you some water." They'd already given her pain medication at the hospital, and the doctor recommended sips of water but no food yet. She honestly felt like she could eat a cow. It had been hours since her last meal.

John returned with the water, helping her take a few sips before putting it on the coffee table in front of them. He sat down at the other end of the couch and lifted her feet onto his lap. His hands played up and down her legs and Katelyn couldn't help but stare at them as they warmed her body. Was that friendly concern or something more? Before she could figure out what it meant, John was back in that cop mode she'd come to recognize. He wasn't outright grilling her. This was his cajoling mode. The one where he tried to convince her she'd seen something when she was little.

"Kate, the only way this makes any sense is if someone is afraid you'll remember something you saw when you were little. Something they can't take a chance on you remembering."

She sighed and tried to draw her legs up to her chest, out of his lap, but he clamped an arm across her ankles and glared at her for a second, then went back to his slow exploration. An exploration that was making her head turn to mush, making it hard to focus on telling him he was crazy with his cold case theories. *Nope. Not a hint of friendly concern in that touch.* Those hands had a mission that had nothing to do with friendship. And if the warm heat building between Katelyn's legs meant anything, her body was fully on board.

"Think about it, Katelyn, why would anyone tell you to leave town if you weren't somehow a threat to them?"

Katelyn shrugged. She didn't really have an answer for him and she was pretty sure she didn't want to talk about this now. "Maybe they wanted to lease the studio space and Charlie leased it to me instead."

That earned her a raised eyebrow.

"I doubt that. The space has been open for over a year. If someone wanted to rent it, they had plenty of time to do that before you came along."

John's hand traveled up her leg, running over her thigh, melting her resolve, along with her panties. *Good heavens.* Katelyn sat up, swinging her legs off John's lap and instantly winced, doubling over at the sharp pain in her head. Her forehead was black and swollen with a small row of six stitches she hoped wouldn't leave a very noticeable scar. Her head was pounding, and nothing seemed capable of settling the storm of waves roiling and thrashing in her stomach.

John was right there, laying her back down again as she fought off the wave of nausea that hit as the pain began to subside.

"Take it easy, Kate. I just think we need to think about

the possibility that your father sent you away for a reason and someone else knows that reason, or at least suspects it. Your mother's killer may very well be living right here in town, and if they are, they're not going to be happy about you being back if there's even the slightest possibility you witnessed her death."

Katelyn wanted to say she wasn't there, that she hadn't witnessed anything, but she hated the fact that the sentences flowed from her as though she'd been trained to say them. John had at least succeeded in planting that seed of doubt. Instead, she mumbled, "Katelyn," and fell back on the couch. Her mother had called her Katelyn. She didn't like it when people shortened her name to Kate.

John simply watched her and waited. The man was infuriating. He set her body on fire with his stupid wandering hands going places they really shouldn't be going, but then never actually following up on the promises they were making. Instead, he grilled her about her mother's murder that she *didn't* witness, and he sat back and waited as though he expected her to crumble under his Jedi stare. As if she would confess some secret memory she'd never told anyone. *Ha!*

Well, it wasn't exactly true. She'd tried to tell her father once, but he didn't listen. He shut her down and told her he didn't want to talk about some made up memory of her mother. She'd also tried to tell her aunt, whose reaction had been the same.

"Urrrr!" Katelyn grunted at John. "Fine. Whatever. I have a memory, but it's not real. I already looked into it."

She felt his hand go still on her legs and she immediately wished they hadn't stopped. She wished she could just ignore all the baggage that came with her coming home, all the complexities of her past. She wished she could just focus on the way her breath became more shallow the more John's hands touched her.

"What do you remember?" he asked, so quiet and coaxing. She hated feeling like he was working her. She smirked at him. Maybe that's what his attention was about. Maybe this was his "hands-on" attempt to get her to talk.

"I told you, it wasn't real. I checked it against the details of the murder scene. It doesn't fit."

John raised an eyebrow, as if to tell her to leave the detective work to him.

"Fine." Katelyn sighed but relented. "But I'm telling you, it doesn't match the scene. I remember hearing my mother scream. That's all."

"And how exactly does that tell you it doesn't match the scene?" John asked.

"In my memory, I'm in a pine forest. I can't see anything. It's completely dark, but I can smell the pine trees all around me. When I was fifteen, I looked up the articles covering my mother's murder. She was found inside Charlie Hanford's office at his house—"

"And, there's not a pine tree or forest anywhere around there," John finished for her. "And she was bludgeoned where she was found," he mumbled to himself, most likely forgetting he was talking about Katelyn's mother's death right in front of her. Katelyn felt her stomach drop at the images his words brought to her mind. They were images she had long tried to keep out of her head but being home had stirred up things again. Stirred up emotions and fears and heartache she wanted to shut away.

"Are we finished now?" she asked. "I want to lie down and nap." *And forget. Forget it all.*

JOHN NODDED, still thinking about what Katelyn had told him. He'd ask her more about it later, but she was right; it didn't fit. John stood and picked Katelyn up in his arms, ignoring the yelp she let out as he lifted her. She felt a little too right in his arms. He fought the urge to cradle her closer, to let his hand slide a little further up her leg, to the soft curve of her ass. His body tightened and hardened in response, not something he wanted to deal with. Not something that should be happening with *this* woman.

Get it together, John.

Gritting his teeth and willing his body into submission, he carried her up to her bed and tucked her in. John slipped each shoe off her foot before covering her with her blanket and then turned out the light.

"I'll wake you in a couple of hours, Kate," he said as he shut the door. A couple of hours should give him time to get himself under control and remind his wayward dick that he couldn't go there.

"Katelyn!" was all he heard in response.

CHAPTER EIGHT

"Hey Kit Kat, time to wake up."

That wasn't the sexy whisper that had woken Katelyn steadily every two hours through the night. When John had roused Katelyn, he'd done it gently, whispering in her ear, rubbing a warm hand down her arm as he sat on the edge of her bed.

She'd hated it. Every time he woke her, he built new fantasies in her head. Dreams where she and John were together and he was waking her for entirely different reasons than looking for signs of concussion. It drove her batty.

Katelyn opened her eyes to see Ashley staring down at her with a big smile on her face. "Hey there, sunshine! I thought you'd never wake up. I was about to call an ambulance, per John's overly-obsessive and not just a little freakishly-cautious instructions."

Katelyn pushed herself up slowly, wincing a little at the

pain in her head. It was much better than the pain she'd felt when she'd gone to bed the night before.

"Ashley? What are you doing here? Where's John?"

As much as he irritated her with all his touchy-feely, making-her-want-him-in-ways-she-shouldn't crap, she realized she missed him when he wasn't there for her. And that, in itself, annoyed her. She wasn't a very needy girl. She liked her independence, her strength. But, she didn't feel very strong right now.

Ashley put a cup of coffee on the nightstand and plopped down on the bed next to her as though they'd been best friends for years. It was a little...disconcerting, but somehow Ashley seemed to make it work.

"He had to go out on an emergency call. There was a car accident up on 190 outside of town. Four cars involved. It's a mess. So, he called me to babysit you." Ashley squinted her eyes and leaned in closer to Katelyn. "Wow, Kit Kat, that's quite a bruise. John said it was bad, but boy did that man understate it."

Katelyn raised a hand to her head and touched the bruised area tenderly. "I must look awful, huh?" Part of her wanted to look in the mirror and find out what she looked like, and part of her wanted to bury her head in bed all day and pretend nothing had happened. If she were honest with herself, the attack had scared her witless. She'd felt safe with John in the house and having Ashley here was preferable to being alone, but she didn't know if she'd get over the fear all that easily. That moment of not knowing what her attacker was going to do to her.... She shivered, and drew the covers up around her.

"Nah," Ashley said, shaking her head. "Not at all, honey. You look... Aw, heck, who am I kidding? You look awful, Kat. Just awful. But don't worry. John doesn't seem to care. The way he went all caveman about you when Cora wanted to set you up with Justin the other night, I'd say you've got him hooked. Regardless of the whole..." Ashley circled her hand around in front of her face as if that said it all.

Katelyn was speechless. She had a feeling Ashley was a bit of an acquired taste, but she felt herself fighting a smile.

"I'm not exactly looking for a relationship right now," she said, then asked herself silently why on earth she was telling this to Ashley.

"Uh-oh. There has to be a bad story behind that one," Ashley said.

Katelyn waved a dismissal. "Not worth telling. Dated for two months, thought it might be going somewhere, he was a married scumbag, yada yada yada."

Ashley's eyes went round. "Oh, no! You had no idea? What a jerk."

"That's what I said. Well, that and a lot more. Anyway, I think I may want to take a break from men for a bit, you know? I'm pretty sure my man-reading radar is broken so I'd rather just sit on the sidelines for a bit."

Liar, said a little voice inside her head.

"Liar," said Ashley. "Besides, John is easily the most honest, straightforward man I know. Not to mention, in a town like this, no one could get away with that. Speaking of, how did he get away with that? How did he fool you that whole time?"

Katelyn winced. Leave it to Ashley to get right to the point. Katelyn just shook her head. "I've been wondering that myself, honestly. I just didn't see the signs. The worst part was, my friends knew. I thought they'd have the kind of response you did, but they didn't. They knew he was married and assumed I did. Who does that?"

"Crazy people. Those crazy city people," Ashley said in a conspiratorial tone and Katelyn had to laugh.

Katelyn picked at the tiny flowers embroidered in the comforter on her bed before giving in to the urge to ask. "When did John say he'd be back?" She should probably go visit her father, but if he saw her like this, he'd have questions and she didn't want to upset him. Then again, how could she avoid him for days or maybe even weeks while her head healed?

"Not sure. At least a few hours, he said. I'll stay, though." Ashley popped off the bed. "I don't cook so I grabbed breakfast on the way over from Two Sisters. Yours is waiting downstairs when you're ready."

"Thanks. Hey, Ashley," Katelyn said as the dark-haired woman started for the door. "What do you do that you were able to just drop everything and come over?" Katelyn didn't know why she wanted to know, but suddenly she was curious.

"Oh, I'm the librarian in town. I locked up and put a sign on the door. I have some volunteers that come by each day. One of them is on her way in to cover. She'll stay if John doesn't get back soon."

Katelyn's jaw dropped. "You're the librarian?"

Ashley laughed. "Someday I'll be offended that everyone gets that look on their face when I tell them what I do. For now, it's just kind of funny."

CHAPTER NINE

J ohn punched in the number for Dr. Max Shapiro, an old colleague from his time in the New York City Police Department. He knew Max would be winding down at the end of his workday and he was hoping to catch him before he left his office.

"'Lo?" came the casual answer at the other end of the phone. John grinned. Max was not your typical psychologist. He wore jeans and sneakers with T-shirts that said things like "Trust me... I'm a therapist" or "I'm sorry your hour is up."

"Hey, Max. It's John Davies," John said, and he could picture the giant bear of a man smiling as a booming "John!" came back at him.

They spent a few minutes catching up, talking about old times without really touching too much on anything happening with his former precinct or buddies. Max worked with a lot of the officers on John's old force, but he understood better than anyone how hard it was for John to relive that time.

"So, I know you didn't call to shoot the breeze. What's up?"

"How much do you know about repressed memories, Max?" John asked. He didn't feel comfortable talking about Katelyn's possible memories with anyone from around Evers. He was hoping Max would be able to tell him what he needed to know.

"I've work with them, some. Is this for a case?"

"I'm not actually sure what I'm dealing with yet. I just wanted to find out more about it. Is it possible for someone to witness something as a child and not remember it at all afterward?"

"It depends who you talk to. For the most part, repressed memories are accepted in the psychiatric community," Max began.

"What about the other part?" John asked.

"Some say they're just made up memories. That they're implanted with suggestive questioning from therapists who don't know what they're doing. Others blame television or books—say people piece together bits of what they've seen in the media and arrange it in their heads until their mind truly believes it happened to them. And, we have no studies yet to show one way or the other. A lot of times there isn't independent corroboration and it's just a 'he-said, she-said' kind of thing."

Max paused for a minute, but John stayed quiet. He knew Max. If he let him keep going, he'd tell him what his gut feeling was. He could almost hear the gears in Max's brain going.

"I'll tell you, though, John. The mind is an incredible thing. If something happens that a person can't handle, the mind is remarkably adept at protecting that person. If a person saw something as a child, something that was too hard for the brain to process, to make sense of, they might have blocked it out right away or it could have happened over time. I don't like the idea of relying on repressed memories as the sole evidence in convicting someone, but it's not a stretch for me to believe that it happens. Not a stretch at all."

John lay a little of Kate's story out for Max. "A woman was killed here twenty-four years ago. Her daughter was four at the time. We've never had reason to believe the daughter witnessed anything, but I'm beginning to have my doubts. She told me she's had small flashes of what she thinks are a memory, but they don't add up with the crime scene. Is it possible she could have seen something and then buried it for this many years?"

"If you're asking for hard evidence, scientific data, I don't have any. If you want my opinion, yes. I believe it's entirely possible," Max said without any hesitation.

"So, even right after the murder, she might not have been able to remember?" John asked. Maybe that's why Alan had never told John that Katelyn witnessed something. Maybe she hadn't been able to tell him anything even right after it happened. It's possible Alan truly believed Katelyn had nothing to tell them—at least, nothing she *could* tell them if the memories were trapped in her head.

"Yes. It's possible she either blocked it out immediately, or she could have been too traumatized to talk about it right away and then, over time, her mind blocked it out."

"Could she have been coached early on about it and not remember the coaching? Every time I ask her about it, her denial is exactly the same: *I didn't see anything. I wasn't there.* Could those lines have been fed to her as a child?"

"It's entirely possible. It could be a combination of her own mind helping her to forget and those around her encouraging the denial."

"Would it be possible for her to have forgotten for this length of time? For twenty-four years?" John asked.

"You bet. And, we never know what will bring out those memories. In one case, a woman remembered witnessing her father kill another little girl when she was six years old. She didn't remember until she was an adult with her own children. Then, the memories began to flash back in bits and pieces," Max said.

John's jaw dropped. "Was she in touch with her father for all of those years?"

"Yep. Raised by him as a child. I'm telling you, the mind protects us. It's an incredible machine. It's why I love what I do so much."

"So, how do I get her to remember what happened?" John asked.

He could hear Max's reluctance over the phone.

"Max, this killer has walked free for twenty-four years. Help me out here, give me something," John said.

"You can talk to a psychiatrist about doing some regression therapy. I can get you some names of people in your area. You don't want to work with just anyone on that kind of thing. Taking her to the scene of the crime might help. Might not."

John cursed. He already knew the scene of the crime didn't match her memory.

"But John, I have to warn you. Her mind is doing this for a reason. I know you want to catch a killer, and I can't tell you what to do, but you need to give some thought to what it could do to her if she remembers whatever she's forgotten. Pushing her on this, pushing to have those memories resurface before she's ready—you could taint the memory by using too much suggestion, or risk harming her beyond what she's already suffered through."

John squeezed his temples as he listened to Max. *Great.* Choose between catching her mother's killer to provide some closure to her dying father, and possibly harming Katelyn irreparably. *Just great.*

"Thanks Max," John said.

"Hey, don't be a stranger. Call if you need anything. Anytime."

John couldn't help but smile. "You too, man. You, too."

John stared at the phone a few minutes longer, then tossed it on the seat next to him. He couldn't talk to his father about this. His dad was retired, but he still bled blue from his time wearing a shield. When John left New York, giving up his gold shield and all he'd accomplished, his dad hadn't understood. Their relationship had taken a hit and it took a long time to heal. He wasn't about to bring up something that would hurt it again.

And, to John's father, there wouldn't be any question. You did what you had to for the sake of a case. Whatever you had to, no matter the cost. John couldn't talk to him about what was going on in his head when he'd left New York, and he couldn't talk to him now. If asked, his father would always choose justice. There was a time when John would have, too.

Nor could he talk to Alan about it. John would have to decide on his own if it was worth pushing Katelyn to remember what she'd seen. If it was worth risking her, risking the case to find the answers he so desperately wanted to give her father.

KATELYN COULDN'T AVOID SEEING her father for very long. She gave herself a day to rest and then convinced John to drive her to the hospital to visit. John was being a hair more overprotective than Katelyn would have liked—he wouldn't let her drive herself yet, for fear she'd get dizzy and have an accident behind the wheel—but she tolerated it because she didn't want him to leave her alone right now. With John on the couch in the living room, she could get a few hours of sleep. If he left her alone at night, she knew the fear would take over and she wouldn't be able to sleep at all.

She didn't know whether to be relieved her father was fully cognizant and seemed to be aware of who she was today or not. In some ways, every visit she had where he was living in the present and able to talk to her was a blessing. On the other hand, maybe it would be easier to convince him her injuries weren't a big deal if he were having one of his off days.

In either case, she wasn't about to tell him what had really happened.

"Katelyn, what happened? Who hurt you?"

That struck Katelyn as an odd way to ask about her injury. The bruising was mostly to the side of her face and forehead. It wasn't the type of black eye you'd see from fists. It could very easily have come from a car accident or fall. Which made her cover story more believable, but her father's question odd.

"Oh, it was nothing, Dad. I had an accident in my car. I didn't see a deer at night and swerved to avoid it. I hit a pole and my head hit the side window. I'm fine, though, really." Katelyn bent and kissed her father's cheek and put the flowers she'd brought in on the windowsill.

Her father didn't answer, but turned to John instead. "John, you'd tell me if anything else was going on, wouldn't you? First she falls down jogging and now this? There anything you need to tell me, son?"

It grated on Katelyn that her father would ask John as if she wasn't even in the room. She wasn't a child, but he never seemed to see that.

John covered for her, but she didn't miss the look he

threw her. And, she knew why. They were both wondering why her father would ask that. Why hadn't he accepted the story of an accident? The only reason not to accept it was if he knew there might be a reason for someone to want to hurt her.

"Nothing to worry about, Alan. She just tangled with a sign post, but we'll get her car taken care of and she'll be good as new in no time. The doctor said she'll have a small scar from the stitches, but that's it."

Katelyn had to admit maybe John's theory that her father sent her away because she saw something when she was young wasn't so crazy after all. Or at least, her father thought she saw something, even though her memories didn't match up with the crime scene. And, now it seemed someone else believed she'd seen something, too.

But how on earth did you defend yourself from a threat based only on the belief that you saw something if you couldn't actually remember?

CHAPTER TEN

Katelyn and John stepped from the room while Alan's nurse changed his sheets and got him cleaned up.

"Coffee?" John asked with a glance toward the elevators that would lead down to the cafeteria.

Katelyn shook her head but smiled. "If I drink another cup, I'll burst. I feel like I've been living on coffee for days now."

By unspoken agreement, they sat on one of the benches spaced out along the hospital corridor. They laughed when they both put their heads back against the wall with a loud sigh at the exact same moment. The strain of coming to the hospital each day was wearing on them.

"How are you managing this? I mean, it's tough on me, but I'm not also running an entire county and taking care of the town's police force."

John turned his head toward her and grinned, those

eyes connecting and holding hers as they always seemed to do. "I have really great guys working for me. They're picking up the slack. Someday, I'll have to pick up the slack for them when they have something going on in their family. It all evens out in the end."

There was a time when Katelyn would have cringed to hear John talk about Alan as his family, but now it soothed her. She'd gotten over her anger, the resentment she'd been holding onto for so long. It felt good, actually. Really, really good to let that go and just lean on John a bit. He was right. It *would* all even out in the end.

The tinny ping of the elevator opening drew both their attention.

"Hi, guys," Katelyn said, stunned to see Shane, Ashley, and an older woman with ghost-white hair carrying a pot of somewhat dilapidated-looking flowers. The poor things were wilting and the petals had all dried up, but that didn't seem to stop the smile on the woman's face as they approached the group.

"Kit Kat, I'd like to introduce you to Ms. Haddie. Hadeline Gertrude Gillman, but everyone in town calls her Haddie," said Shane.

Katelyn threw a glare to Ashley over the spreading of the nickname, before quickly smiling at Haddie and shaking her hand.

"It's so nice to meet you, Ms. Haddie. I'm Katelyn."

"Hello, Kit Kat. We've come to bring flowers for your father," came Haddie's response, drawing a quick burst of laughter from Ashley. Katelyn just shook her head as

Haddie continued. "Flowers are quite good for the soul, you know."

"You bet they are, ma'am. Let me hold those for you," John said as he reached for the potted plant.

"It's so nice of you all to come by. My dad will be happy to see you. The nurse is in with him now, but she'll be out soon."

"We don't want to take up your visiting time with him, if you haven't been in to see him yet," Shane offered with a glance at the closed door to Alan's room.

"Oh, no. He'll be happy to see fresh faces. We've been here all morning," Katelyn said, a bit puzzled at the look on Haddie's face. As Katelyn spoke to Shane, Haddie stared at Katelyn making her squirm a little under the scrutiny. It didn't take long to figure out why.

"It really is uncanny. The spitting image, you are. Absolute mirror image," Haddie said, turning to Ashley as though she expected Ashley to agree with her, but Ashley simply shook her head and shrugged at Shane.

Haddie turned back to Katelyn. "I bet you're just as sweet as your mother was, too, aren't you?"

"You knew my mother?" Katelyn asked, not able to hold the smile back. It hadn't occurred to her that there would be people who knew her mother. Who remembered not just the tragic way she died, but who she was when she was alive.

"Sure did. Sweetest little thing and boy, could she bake," Haddie said, but John broke in.

"Katelyn's a little prickly. Don't know that I'd call her

107

sweet. And she hasn't baked a damn thing for me yet," John joked, earning an elbow to the ribs from Katelyn and a smack on the forearm from Haddie.

"Oh, my," Haddie said, caressing the muscles in John's arm. "My, my, my."

"Haddie! Behave yourself or I'll take you right back to the library," Ashley said, but her smile cut the threat. "Haddie volunteers with me at the library most days. It's a way to keep her out of trouble. And, Shane comes to get us for lunch sometimes since his law office is just across the street."

Katelyn tipped her head and looked at Ashley sideways. "*You're* Haddie's way of keeping out of trouble. That's rich."

Ashley just grinned.

"Did you find a new paralegal yet, Shane?" John asked.

"No, nothing yet. I'm getting desperate. The only people I've had apply were a guy who said he felt a cosmic connection with me and knew we'd work together like two peas in a pod—literally, he said those exact words during the interview—and a woman who lied about four of the five jobs on her resume. She really did work at JJ's Drive Thru Burgers in high school, if that counts for anything, though."

Shane glared as Ashley nearly busted a gut laughing at him. Katelyn fought back laughter but couldn't keep the grin off her face. The group continued to chat with Haddie and Katelyn sitting on the bench together and Ashley and the men standing until the nurse came out a few minutes later.

"You guys go on in," Katelyn said. "We'll go grab a cup of coffee and come back in a few minutes."

"Are you sure? We can wait if you want," Shane offered, but John and Katelyn shooed them into the room before walking toward the elevator.

"Are Shane and Ashley dating?" Katelyn asked as the doors shut and the elevator started its descent.

"No, why?" John's answer sounded a little defensive, drawing another smile from Katelyn. She was doing a lot more of that these days. Smiling.

"I just wondered since she said he comes to take her to lunch sometimes."

"Oh, yeah, that," John said, sounding somewhat mollified. He shrugged. "They just hang out a lot. They both work in town and they went to high school together. I think they may have dated briefly in high school, but nothing major. As far as I know, they're just friends now."

Ashley, Shane, and Haddie were leaving her father's room when Katelyn and John got back a few minutes later with their coffee in hand. Haddie seemed a bit sad and shaken by the visit, so they said their goodbyes as Ashley and Shane got her into the elevator. Katelyn understood. It wasn't easy seeing her father reduced to this. It wasn't easy at all.

"I HAVE the rest of the day off. How about letting me take you to lunch?" John took Katelyn's hand in his as they walked out of the hospital and the touch sensitized her entire body instantly. "We can have the sisters wrap some food up and take it out to the lake. Perfect day for a picnic."

John smiled that melt-your-heart grin of his, but Katelyn pulled back, stopping him. "Why are you doing this, John?"

He looked at her, confusion evident on his face.

Does he really not know? "This." Katelyn waved her arm between the two of them, flustered that she'd spoken up. She should have kept quiet and ignored...whatever it was he was doing.

John tilted his head. "This, what?" he asked, mimicking her arm wave.

"You know what. This, whatever it is you're doing, treating me like...like..." Red burned up the sides of Katelyn's face and she knew she had to look like a damn apple. A very unattractive blotchy apple. She couldn't bring herself to say he was treating her like he liked her.

What if he was only trying to be nice, and now I'm making a fool out of myself by letting him know I'm taking it the wrong way? The incident with Devan had really screwed with her head. Katelyn didn't think she could mistake the signs John was sending her for concerned friendliness any longer, but she was also much too leery of relying on her instincts after Devan. She'd never felt so much self-doubt. She hated it.

John stepped into her and looped one arm around her waist, pulling her into him, brushing her body with the hard front of his chest, the press of his thighs against her, the...*oh my.*

"Treating you like I like you?" he asked. His words came as a rough whisper that stole the little breath she had left.

Nope. Not imagining that, Katelyn thought, with the tiny piece of her brain that hadn't dissolved yet.

"Yes," Katelyn whispered. "That."

John's other hand ran down the back of her arm, sending a shiver through her. How could she have thought she was imagining *this*? "I'm treating you like I like you because I do. I know I shouldn't. You're Alan's daughter, a potential witness in a case. I should be looking for distance, but I can't. I like you, Katelyn. A lot."

The corners of his mouth turned up and his voice was husky and low. It walked right up her spine when he spoke, sending that shiver from the top of her head to the tips of her fingers and toes.

The blare of a car horn broke the moment just as Katelyn was sure John was going to kiss her. Oh, how she wanted that kiss. She didn't know what had happened to the John she loved to hate, to all those feelings of resentment she'd been building up and saving just to lash out at him. They were gone. They'd just fizzled out and were lying unwanted in a closet in her mind or some such empty space. They were right next to her feelings of mistrust over men after finding out the snake was married, but if there was one thing John wasn't, it was dishonest. That much she knew. And, right here, right now, she wanted nothing but this man.

Katelyn glared at the car, but John just chuckled and waved back at the old guy waving at him as he drove by.

John turned to Katelyn and trapped her fingers between his, lacing their hands together and tugging her toward his car. "Come on. Let me take you on a picnic."

She followed along, but still wished she knew how that kiss would have turned out. "There are going to be rumors all over town tomorrow that we were practically having sex in the parking lot of the hospital, aren't there?"

"You're catching on to this town, huh?" John laughed and Katelyn just shook her head.

And two hours later, she was just as frustrated and let down as she had been in the parking lot.

Are you kidding me? They were in a secluded, romantic spot by the water without another soul around. They talked about everything and nothing. They laughed and teased each other. They ate way too much food. Everything from chicken salad to peach cobbler, packed by the sisters. John held her hand, let his fingers brush her arm or the back of her neck as they talked, and even traced circles on her stomach as they lay on a blanket stretched out next to each other. But, he hadn't kissed her yet. And Katelyn was just about ready to burst.

"Tell me more about your sculptures, Katelyn. Why do you work with metal? Why not stone or, I don't know...wood?"

At the moment, Katelyn's brain was primarily a mixture of mush and sweet, puffy clouds. At least that's what it felt like every time John traced another one of his circles. The heat pooling low in her hips and stomach didn't leave a whole lot of room for coherent thought and conversation at this point.

"Umm, what?" she asked, somewhat dazed as she stared at his hand tracing its pattern.

Damn him. He knows perfectly well what he's doing to me.

John smiled that wicked grin he had when he was up to something. "I'm glad you came home, Katelyn," he said, his hand now still on her stomach spreading heat through her whole body, making her tingle with anticipation.

"I'm beginning to be pretty happy about that, too," she said with a smile as her eyes dropped to his mouth again. She had a really hard time not focusing on his mouth. He had really full lips that somehow looked like they'd be both firm and soft at the same time. They made her want to lean up and lick them. Just the tiniest little bit. Nothing more than a little flick with her tongue to see what he'd do.

Her breath caught as she let her fantasy take over, but a split second before she acted on her thoughts, John laughed. Deep and low and so knowing. As if he knew what he'd been doing to her all this time. How he was teasing her.

John leaned in close, almost touching his mouth with hers, but leaving the smallest of margins. He was teasing her. Well, she could tease, too. She moved just a hair closer to him, rolled in and put her hands on his chest.

Rock hard. But, warm and oh, so much better than rock. Katelyn couldn't breathe as she slid her hands over the thin fabric of his T-shirt, pulled taut over hard lines and sculpted muscles. She wondered briefly if she'd pass out from holding her breath before they had a chance to kiss.

She let herself look up. That might have been a mistake. When she met his eyes, she was utterly lost in the intensity of what she saw reflected there. There was heat and lust and need.

John stilled for a minute, then wrapped his arms around her, trapping her against him. He crushed her to him so deliciously, she never wanted to break the connection. And then his mouth was on hers, and it wasn't slow or gentle or questioning. It was all-encompassing. John kissed the way he did everything in life. All out. All or nothing. And Katelyn wanted to give him nothing less.

She slid her arms up his chest and looped them around his neck, pulling him ever closer as his tongue swept hers. Every part of her body was responding to his demands, and Katelyn forgot about any ideas of taking a break from men.

But two seconds later, a deafening crack cut the air. John moved faster than lightning, pinning her beneath him on the ground. The John she'd been kissing was gone and Sheriff John Davies, unyielding and all business, was in his place. Confusion swamped Katelyn. *Was that really a gunshot?* She had no idea when hunting season was or whether hunters would be allowed so close to an area that had walkers and hikers and boaters on the weekends. It didn't seem like there should be anyone shooting so close to them.

"Stay behind me," John said, as he moved into a crouch and pushed her down behind him. They moved quickly to his cruiser. He reached in his pocket. Katelyn heard the tell-tale beeps and clicks of the key fob, and doors unlocking. John pulled open the passenger door of the car and grabbed a long rifle out of its rack between the two front seats.

"Don't move," he ordered as he pressed her against the side of the car. She had no idea what he was doing. Knowing him, he was going to run off into the woods. Chase down the shooter, then give them a ticket for hunting without a license or hunting in an undesignated area or something official like that. Another shot rang out. Katelyn ducked. This time, she had actually seen the bullet hit the dirt a few yards behind and to the side of the car. *That* seemed a little too close. What the heck was this person hunting? As Katelyn saw John raise the scope of the very long rifle to his eye and scan the woods, it dawned on her.

Us. They're hunting us.

John hadn't seen the muzzle blast of the first shot because he'd been too busy doing what he did best—screwing around with a witness to a crime instead of protecting her the way he should be. In that instant, he'd flashed back to New York. To the sight of Lexi Ambrose's dead body as it was dumped beaten and lifeless outside the police precinct with his name written in her own blood across her chest.

When the second shot came, he'd been scanning the woods. He'd seen the muzzle blast. But as he looked through the scope of his rifle a mere second later, the shooter was nowhere in sight. *Nothing. Damn it.* Whoever it was knew how to blend into these woods and how to move quickly. Chances were they also knew which way to go to get out of the area before he could track them or get any of his men here from town.

John searched again, widening the area, knowing the person would have moved by now. Most likely, they retreated straight back, making it impossible to see them if he wanted to stay with Katelyn and protect her. John moved to the front of the vehicle, checking quickly on Katelyn before calling in the shots. He cursed under his breath.

He had stupidly had her right out in the open, and neither had been paying any attention to who might be around. He'd been so damned lost in her, in that kiss. Never again. He'd barely been able to live with himself the first time he got a witness killed. He couldn't let it happen with again. Time to get his head back in the game and track this killer. Twenty-four years was too damned long for a murderer to be on the loose.

CHAPTER ELEVEN

The car ride back to Katelyn's house was tense and silent. John had made her wait in the car while he spoke to his deputies who'd arrived on the scene within minutes of getting his call for backup. John had looked angry and dangerous as she watched him through the window.

Katelyn didn't want an angry, dangerous lawman by her side right now. She wanted John. The way he'd been by her side through all of the talks with her father's doctors, throughout all of her adjustment to coming home. She wanted supportive-caring John—not scary-serious John who was so rigid he didn't talk to her.

When they neared her house, Katelyn finally broke the silence. "Are you going to tell me what happened back there? Was someone really shooting at us or was it just some idiot who doesn't know where and when he's allowed to hunt?"

John didn't answer right away. He pulled into her father's driveway and turned off the engine then radioed for a cruiser to watch her house.

Great. A babysitter.

John turned to her before speaking, one arm resting on the steering wheel, the other laying on the seat between them. He didn't reach for her. It was as if he'd put up a wall. And, apparently, it was a wall he wouldn't be crossing.

"They were shooting at us. I don't think the shooter meant to hit us. Whoever it was, they had plenty of time to line up that shot. We were pretty exposed out there. I think someone's still trying to get you to leave town."

Katelyn swallowed. "I'm not leaving again. I'm not going anywhere." She could feel the thickness building in her throat as she fought back rising panic. She wouldn't be chased away again. She'd had no say in things as a child and, even as an adult, she'd let her father convince her to stay in Austin. Not anymore. She wouldn't leave this time.

"I know, Kate. But whoever this is, they're escalating, and I won't take chances with your life. We can't have you out in the open again. Not for now, at least."

"Where are you going?" she asked. It was obvious he had no intention of coming inside with her.

He didn't answer but exited the car and came around to open her door.

When they were on the porch, she tried again.

"Where are you going, John?" she asked more forcefully this time. Did he think he could just blow her off now or treat her like a child the way her father always had? Katelyn was damn tired of no one asking her opinion, of people telling her what she could do and where she could go. She was tired of people sending her away. And that's exactly what it felt like John was doing. Pushing her away.

"I just have some things to do," he said, not meeting her eyes.

"John..."

He cut her off with a hard look. His eyes were flat and lifeless. They sent a chill right through her. He wasn't reachable right now.

She woodenly promised not to open the door for anyone other than John or Danny in response to his barked commands, then let herself inside and closed the door. She watched through the window as he walked back to his cruiser without so much as a glance back over his shoulder.

JOHN HATED the look on Katelyn's face when he dropped her at her house. She knew he was pulling away from her, but it couldn't be helped. He'd been an idiot to think getting involved with her was okay. At least he could stop now before it was too late. He needed to focus on catching whoever had killed her mom, whoever was coming after her now. If he could do that, then maybe—if she didn't hate his guts by then—he could see if there was anything worth pursuing left between them.

He waited in his cruiser until one of his deputies arrived at the house then went straight to the hospital. It was time someone in this case started talking, and he knew damn well Alan Bowden knew more than he'd been telling all these years.

John cursed as soon as he walked in the room. The slack look on Alan's face told him this wouldn't be a very lucid visit. There was no telling what decade his former mentor thought it was.

Before John could say a word, anger sparked in Alan's eyes. "What are you doing here again? I gave you an order to get back to work. Do you think this damn town is going to run itself if you keep lazing around here? I need someone I can trust on duty until I get out of this damn place." Alan struck the side rail on his bed for emphasis as he glared at what he no doubt thought was his young deputy, not the new sheriff. The irony was, when Alan was sheriff, he'd never talked to any of his deputies this way. He was stern, but always fair. He led well and demanded respect, but gave it equally.

The dementia brought out anger and a mean streak no one had seen coming. The doctor had said to expect it, but that didn't make it any less shocking.

John pressed on. Whether Alan was living in this year or not, he had to get him to talk if he was going to keep Katelyn safe.

"I'm here about Caroline's case, Alan," John said and he stood next to the bed rather than sitting. He needed to interrogate his mentor, not coddle him now.

Alan blanched but he didn't reply, and John wasn't sure if he'd just pulled him back to the present or not. "Alan, you need to tell me what Katelyn saw. What she witnessed that made you send her away."

That got Alan's attention. "Don't bring Katelyn into this. You listen to me," Alan tried to sit up, his face quickly turning red with the effort. Machines beeped alerts to the nurses down the hall. "You can't bring Katelyn here. You leave her be where she is, John—where she's safe." His eyes were wild with desperation.

John knew he wasn't in the present. He seemed to have no idea Katelyn had moved to Evers.

The door burst open and a nurse crowded the room, trying to push John out as she silenced the alarm and urged Alan to lie back down. John shoved closer. "She's already here, Alan, and from the looks of it, someone's coming after her. You need to tell me what she saw so I can stop whoever's doing this."

It was useless. Alan shook his head and continued to insist John get Katelyn out of town. John felt hopeless as he let the nurse push him out of the room. How could he protect Katelyn if she couldn't remember what happened, and Alan wouldn't tell him what she'd seen or even where she was when her mother was murdered? Had she witnessed the murder itself or did she see or hear something afterward that Alan thought might get her hurt? But, if that were the case, why would Alan hide it from John, of all people?

He wanted to hit the hallway wall, throwing all his frustration into beating something that couldn't fight back.

That's how he felt. Like he couldn't fight back. There were no leads and nothing to go on.

Except what had happened today. John radioed into Berta.

"Yeah, boss?" came the scratchy voice.

"Is Carter back yet?" He'd sent Carter Jenkins, one of his younger deputies, out to the woods where he and Katelyn were shot at to scour the area for any evidence. Carter might be young, but he had grown up in the area and knew how to hunt and track. If anyone could follow the shooter or find a piece of evidence out there, it would be Carter.

"No. On his way in, though. He radioed a few minutes ago and said he's got fresh tire tracks but nothing much useful. Tread is similar to any you'd find on a truck out here."

John groaned. Most of the men and half the grandmothers in the area drove a truck. "Did he get the tread just in case?"

"Yup. Took an impression. That's all he found."

John needed time to think. Leaving the hospital, he turned right and headed out of town toward Bishop Ranch. The twenty-minute drive wasn't fun. There was nothing to do but stew on the fact that someone was coming for Katelyn and he didn't have a clue who it was or how to stop them.

When he got to the ranch, he didn't stop at the horse barn or the house. He looped around past Laura Bishop's greenhouses and took the road to the old barn. Cade Bishop would probably come say hi and try to see what was bothering John eventually, but he'd likely give him a little while to work things out first. John parked by the barn and climbed up to the hayloft-turned-gym. Cade and Shane's dad had closed in the hayloft and put in punching bags and some free weights when the brothers were teenagers. The setup offered privacy he couldn't get at his gym. John took them up on their invitation to use it every once in a while when his demons got too close.

He taped up his hands and slipped on gloves, turning to the heavy bag as images of Katelyn filled his mind. They weren't the images he wanted of her in his head. They were pictures of her lifeless body with a bullet hole through her chest and his name written in blood just as it had been on Lexi. The kind of dread he was filled with now was the same feeling he'd had when Lexi wasn't answering his calls. When word on the street said his cover was blown and Lexi had been labeled a snitch.

John hit the bag over and over trying to make the reel in his head stop playing, but nothing could fix this for him. No amount of physical exertion was going to stop what he saw in his mind's eye. He had to find a way to solve the mystery of Caroline's murder or turn up a lead on who was coming after Katelyn now.

It wasn't Cade who came up to find him after all. John heard May Bishop's voice call up the stairs and dropped his arms. He couldn't just ignore her the way he might have with Cade.

"John, you know I can't climb those stairs. You can't

leave an old lady down here waiting for you. Come on down."

"Yes, ma'am. Coming," John said as he used his arm to wipe sweat from his brow. He worked the gloves and tape off his hands, then grabbed a towel and bottle of water before taking the stairs as slowly as he could. He felt like a child being taken to task by his mother. She'd want him to talk and May Bishop always got her way.

John tilted his head from side to side, trying to stretch the tension out of his neck before finally taking the last step. May sat patiently in her wheelchair near what used to be her husband's workbench. This barn had been his "Tinker Barn," the place where Cade and Shane's father worked on all of his inventions. One of which had given the Bishops the money they all lived off today, an industrial glue used all over the world in manufacturing.

"Did Cade rat me out?" John asked, almost petulantly.

"Hummph!" May laughed a response of sorts. "Cade and Shane used this place all the time when they were kids. Always needing to blow off steam or work something out. Nowadays, they don't seem to need it much at all. So, when they do come out here, I know it's something big bothering them. Something that's knocked 'em on their butts good. I'd imagine it's the same with you. You're a pretty even-keeled guy these days. What came along and knocked you down?"

John shrugged. He felt like a kid, not wanting to talk, but wanting to all at once. Almost hoping she'd pull it out of him so he could get this off his chest, but not quite knowing how to start the conversation.

She wheeled over to an old table and pointed at a chair. "Plant it and tell me what's got you out here."

"Not much to tell. I'm pretty sure Alan sent his daughter away years ago because she witnessed her mother's murder, only her memories don't make sense given what we know about the crime scene. And what little she does remember doesn't tell me anything about who killed her mom. But someone in town doesn't seem to care about that. They came after Katelyn and roughed her up, and now they're shooting at her."

May's eyes went wide, and John realized he should have expanded on that a bit more.

"She's all right," he said quickly to set May at ease, "but I don't have any leads and Alan refuses to tell me what he knows. I don't have any way to keep her safe. Other than sending her back to Austin, and who knows if that will really keep her safe this time. Now that this person suspects she knows something, they may go after her even if she leaves town."

"And you don't exactly want to send her away, do you?" May asked. She had an annoying way of seeing right through a person. John didn't know if it was voodoo magic or witchcraft, but the woman knew and saw all—somehow.

John didn't answer. He met May's eyes and waited. She merely raised her brows and waited right back.

John relented. "It doesn't matter what I want. If I get emotionally involved, I'll get her killed," he said, studying the dirt packed into the floorboards of the barn.

"Like New York?"

John's head shot up. *Voodoo.* Alan was the only one—should be the only one—who knew about New York.

May smiled that innocent sweet smile she used when she was about to tell someone what they needed to do to fix their world. "My Jim was good friends with Alan back in the day. He probably shouldn't have shared your story, but Alan wanted some advice when he was hiring that year. Wanted to know if we thought you were too broken to do the job."

She said this very matter-of-factly, but the truth was, he probably had been too broken. He'd always thought Alan Bowden had been nuts to take a gamble on him.

When he came here from New York, he'd been one of the youngest police detectives in New York City, but he'd earned that badge the hard way, by doing undercover work in one of the city's most ruthless gangs. He took down a lot of people in the end, but his informant paid with her life and John paid with his soul. It took Alan Bowden a long time to convince John life was still worth living. That he could still be a good man, lead a good life, and not let the guilt of what had happened eat him alive.

"You weren't too broken then and you're not now. You're just doubting yourself," May said quietly, her eyes boring a hole in him.

"I let myself get distracted again, May. Just like I did with Lexi. I got Lexi killed and I'm about to do the same thing to Katelyn."

May shook her head sadly but her eyes were fierce. "You did no such thing, young man."

John tried to let that sink in as she dressed him down like he was one of her own boys. He figured Cade and Shane had been on the receiving end of this more than once. "I almost got her shot today, May!"

"I'd be willing to bet it wasn't your fault she almost got shot. What do you expect of yourself, John? Do you think you should keep her under lock and key at all times? With an armed guard outside her house? That you should be with her twenty-four seven? That you should have predicted the exact time and location of the shooting and prevented it somehow? What superhuman thing is it that you should have done? Because I got news for you, John. You can't keep everyone safe all the time." She barely seemed to take a breath as John stood, stunned into silence.

"And I'll tell you something else—you didn't get Lexi killed. That gang killed Lexi. Her circumstances and her own choices before you connected with her weren't the best, so that didn't help matters any, but you didn't kill her, John. Criminals did that. You brought them to justice, that's all. And you won't get Katelyn killed either. You and your men can keep her safe until you can find out who's doing this to her."

John looked back at May, wanting to believe her, but doubt still swirled in his mind and his heart.

"You can't take the world on your shoulders, John. You'll crumble if you try. This person who's doing these things, they've hidden for over twenty years. They're coming out of whatever hole they've been hiding in. That means they'll make a mistake, eventually. They'll leave a trail for you to follow somewhere along the way. When they slip up, you'll get them. You just keep Katelyn close to you until then. Pull her close and keep her safe with you instead of pushing her away. Heaven knows that child has been pushed away long enough."

May turned and pushed herself back along the paved pathway, one of many that webbed the farm to allow her to get around in her chair. She was muttering something about foolish men making foolish choices. He didn't know if she was talking about him or the choice Alan had made to send Katelyn away and keep her away all these years. Probably both.

John saw Josh Samuels, Shane and Cade's likely future stepfather, walk out of the shadows and push May's chair back up to the house for her. What he wouldn't give to have the kind of love those two had.

It took about two seconds for John to realize May was right. He needed to talk to Kate. Try to explain. Then he'd let her decide if she wanted to take the risk, whether she thought he could keep her safe if they were involved. Katelyn would understand. But, he had a feeling she wouldn't want to let ghosts rule her any longer. Whether it was Lexi's ghost or her mother's ghost, John knew Katelyn wouldn't want any of them getting in the way of her living her own life. And, neither did he.

CHAPTER TWELVE

Katelyn paced the kitchen. Normally, when she was upset she'd go to the studio and lose herself in her art. That wasn't possible right now. Her studio was still being built, and all of her art and supplies were packed away in storage boxes in her car and her father's dining room. She thought about cooking, but the refrigerator and freezer were already filled to capacity with casseroles and cakes and salads from her neighbors who insisted on feeding her while her father was ill.

Katelyn sighed. She should be grateful to them. She *was* grateful. But she was also irritated, aggravated, annoyed, and pretty damned ticked off at this point. At John, if she was honest. Not her neighbors.

If he would just get back here, she could vent her frustration...no, it was anger really. She could vent her anger where it belonged—on him. He was pushing her away. The only thing she couldn't figure out was why.

But the *why* didn't matter. Katelyn had lived her whole life letting her father push her away and she was tired of it. Whatever was going on in John's head, she'd just tell him to stop it.

Sure...that oughta work, Katelyn. Good plan.

Katelyn huffed out a breath and tossed herself down in a chair to wait.

She popped back up again. Pacing was better. Moving would let her keep up a good head of steam to spew at John when he came back.

The sound of a car door closing pulled her from her thoughts. She heard the front door open and murmured conversation in the living room between John and the deputy who had been babysitting her. Katelyn braced herself in the kitchen. She'd just wait for him to come in and then tell him how this was going to go. She'd tell him she wouldn't stand for him pulling away whenever he wanted to. That whatever was going through his head was...well, she really didn't know what was going through his head so she had no idea what she'd say. But, she'd say something, dammit.

The look on his face when he walked into the kitchen stopped Katelyn short. He looked positively wrecked. The man in front of her was utterly destroyed. Katelyn looped her arms around his neck and pulled him down to her, resting her forehead on his. She needed to be close to him, to feel him and know he could feel her.

"What is it?" she whispered.

John didn't answer. He lifted her into his arms and

carried her to the couch, holding her tight to him as though he'd never let her go. And, Katelyn realized, she never wanted him to let go. The feeling of being in his arms felt right, as though everything that was messed up in her world was suddenly okay. Or, at least, didn't matter very much. With his arms around her, Katelyn could ignore all the stress and the fear, and the questions and doubts. She could let herself just be.

John sat on the couch with Katelyn in his lap and leaned back. He held her for a long time before speaking.

"Sorry, I freaked and ran," he finally said.

Katelyn looked into his eyes. She'd always been drawn to them. They weren't quite brown, or clearly green. They were some mixture of both colors that mesmerized her and made her want to sink into them for hours. Made her want to lose herself in them. When he had shuttered his eyes from her earlier, it had scared her. The fact that he would hide himself from her freaked her out.

"What happened?" she asked, somehow knowing the answer wouldn't have anything to do with today.

"Did your dad ever tell you anything about my background when I came to work for him?"

Katelyn shook her head. Only his slight accent told her he was from New York. Other than that, she didn't know anything about his background. It hadn't struck her as odd until now that her father hadn't said anything. He talked about John all the time and yet, as she thought back, she couldn't remember a single story about John's past.

"I worked undercover in New York City before I came

here. Eighteen months deep undercover in one of the sickest gangs New York had ever seen. I worked my way through the ranks getting close to the leader, Eddie Coleman; a crazy bastard who ruled his turf by killing anyone who got in his way in the most twisted ways he could come up with."

Katelyn felt a shiver run through John. She lay her head on his shoulder and held him as he kept talking, his hands running up and down her back as he spoke.

"I always wanted to be a cop, and I never really gave much thought to the danger I'd put myself in to catch this guy. We needed evidence we could use to get him off the streets for good. And I was okay with putting myself at risk to do that." The deep breath John took felt as if he had to work to take it, like the life he was remembering was choking him. "I got close to one of the girls who hung out with the gang. Girls were passed around from member to member—group property. But, if a guy was strong enough, if his position was solid enough in the gang, he could claim a girl as his property only."

His words and tone were bitter, and she could tell the thought of having to claim a woman as his property sickened him. It sickened her. Katelyn held herself still, careful not to flinch. She couldn't imagine John living in that world, having to immerse himself in it for any reason. Justice and doing what was right were such innate parts of who he was. She could tell he was sinking back into that life as he talked. The slight New York accent she hardly ever heard became more pronounced.

"I claimed Lexi. Technically, Eddie could still touch her if he wanted to, but no one else could. She gave me information, told me things she overheard when no one thought she was listening." John paused for a long time, as though gathering himself.

"One day, I was hanging out at Eddie's house with a bunch of the guys and I got this bad feeling. We were set to take down the whole gang in the next few days. We were just waiting on some warrants. But I got this feeling, like everyone was looking at me funny and no one wanted to let me leave. I kept texting Lexi but she wasn't answering."

John seemed lost, reliving the story, and Katelyn was frozen in his arms. The tension coursing through his body was palpable, his muscles taut and unyielding beneath her.

"All of a sudden, everyone was fine with me leaving, but they had these big smiles on their faces and I knew something was wrong. The whole way to my car, I thought I'd be shot in the back any minute. I thought they'd made me and I wasn't going to get out of there alive. But nothing happened. They let me drive away. I went to Lexi's apartment but she wasn't there. I drove to all the places she might be, but I couldn't find her. I looked for hours. Then, I got to the station and heard about the rumors. My cover had been blown. Lexi had been labeled a snitch. I'm not there for two minutes before there's a whole lot of noise out front."

John didn't speak again for a while. Katelyn waited. The tension in her body matched his with the dread of knowing what was coming. Whatever it was would be horrible and she didn't want to hear it, but she would. For

John, she'd listen and help him through it, because it obviously affected what he was feeling about her at the moment.

"I let myself get distracted by Lexi. I wasn't focused. I should have focused on the job," John all but whispered. "They dumped her body out in front of the police station like she was trash." His voice was thick with unshed tears.

Katelyn took his head in her hands, forcing him to look at her. "I'm not Lexi, honey. I'm not her, and we're not caught in the crossfire of a gang war."

John's voice cracked when he answered. She could hear the pain seeping in no matter how hard he tried to cover it. "What if I lose focus? What if I lose you?" he asked.

Katelyn framed his face with her hands and kissed him softly. "You won't," she said against his lips. "You won't lose me."

He wrapped himself around her, kissing her with drugging kisses that stoked the fire burning inside her. But, tonight wasn't about that fire. It was about comfort and connection. About simply being together, holding on.

Hours later, he walked her up to her bed and went back downstairs to sleep on the couch. Katelyn didn't sleep for a long time. Her mind raced with thoughts of the man who was guarding her, thoughts of the man she knew would do anything to protect her. With no memory of what she'd witnessed as a child, Katelyn was powerless to help him figure out who was coming after her. Who was putting them both in harm's way.

CHAPTER THIRTEEN

J ohn stared at the big house at the top of Evers Hill on
the edge of town. It was easily twenty times larger
than any single man needed, but as a developer, it
was Charlie Hanford's pride and joy. He threw an annual
holiday party there that anyone in any kind of position in
town was invited to, complete with valet parking and
personalized Christmas trinkets for each guest. The party
was gaudy as heck, but it was all Charlie.

The house had also been the scene of Caroline
Bowden's murder. John wondered why Charlie Hanford
hadn't moved out after it happened. His best friend's wife
had been killed in his office, yet he still worked at that desk
every day. What on earth would possess a man to do that?

Arrogance, came the answer. Charlie was too arrogant
to give up his house on the hill even after finding Caroline
murdered there.

He sat in his cruiser, staring at the house. He'd driven to

each of the neighbors' houses and checked the angles. Because of the hill and the way the driveway curved, neither neighbor had a very good view of the top of the drive. It would have been hard to see much more than a general description of a car parked up there.

Unless Marcy Whorton had driven past at the precise moment the red truck drove up the driveway, she wouldn't have seen much. Danny had left for Sol City—the large retirement community outside of town—this morning to see if Marcy remembered what she'd seen the day of Caroline's murder. John headed back into town as he waited for a call from Danny. The radio crackled to life as he pulled into one of the slanted parking spots in front of Two Sisters Diner.

"Boss?"

"Yeah, Danny? What have you got?" John asked, not opening his car door. He didn't want anyone to overhear this conversation.

"Marcy Whorton is here all right, and she remembers everything about that day. She's pretty, um, spunky, I guess you could call her, boss."

John would have laughed if the information he needed wasn't so serious. Danny was often fighting off advances from older women. *Much* older women.

"What'd she remember?"

"She says she only told the officer she'd seen a red truck. She told him she couldn't tell him anything more about it. Didn't see a plate, the driver, how new or old it was. Nothing. But get this, boss. She says it was Sam Denton who put the idea in the officer's head that it was Ken Statler. They were all standing outside the front of the house. By that time, everyone in town that could get to Charlie's place was standing at the bottom of the driveway where the police had the area blocked off. She went over to tell the officer what she saw, and Sam and Charlie were standing there next to her. She remembers it was Sam who said, 'that would've been Ken Statler's truck' as though he knew Ken had been there. She said the officer wrote it down and that was that."

John didn't answer right away. He was too busy cursing under his breath at the officer who didn't follow up, didn't confirm one way or the other whose truck was outside the house that day. And there had never been any confirmation of an alibi for Ken Statler. He'd simply disappeared so no one had a chance to find out where he'd been that day.

"Thanks, Danny. Come on back. We'll go see Marcy again if we come up with anything else."

As John stared through the window of his cruiser, he could only think one thing. Sam Denton seemed to be circling around a lot of the details of this mystery. He had supposedly been with Charlie moments before Charlie discovered Caroline's body. The police report stated the two had met in Charlie's living room to exchange some papers and then Sam had left. Charlie went into the office and found Caroline. If it was really Sam's truck in the driveway, not Ken Statler's, could Sam have been there earlier in the day and Charlie didn't know it?

John's mind scrolled back over the details of the day Caroline was killed. He pulled Charlie's statement out of his memory and went back over the facts. Charlie said he had arrived to meet with Sam and Sam was waiting for him. They reviewed some papers in the living room, then Sam left before Charlie found Caroline. Sam Denton's fingerprints were found in Charlie's office, but they had been on the list of prints that were expected to be found in there, along with Charlie's, Caroline's, and Charlie's cleaning woman's.

John thought back to all the other facts in his head that were connected to Sam Denton. When Katelyn was attacked last week, John had asked the guys working on the build-out at her studio if they'd seen anyone around the day of her attack, or in the days leading up to it, who shouldn't have been there. Sam gave a vague description of a car. Dark sedan, a little beat up. The kind of car you might see in a hundred or more driveways around here. Oddly, no one else had seen the car. Only Sam.

John felt sick to his stomach as he wondered if the answer to this mystery had been right under their noses, so damn close to home all these years. The biggest problem he'd have would be finding an actual answer. He definitely didn't have enough for a warrant. If he brought Sam in to question him, he'd tip him off that he was suspicious and any evidence that might exist in this twenty-four-year-old mystery would be destroyed—if it hadn't been already.

John forgot about lunch as he pulled out of the parking spot and headed toward the hospital. He hoped like hell he'd find Alan awake and cognizant today of all days.

~

A NURSE SMILED at John as he entered Alan's hospital room. "He's a little worn out today, I'm afraid," she said as she let herself out with a sympathetic look at Alan, who lay sleeping in the bed.

John winced. He knew Alan's condition was getting worse, but he wasn't ready to face that reality yet. He pulled a chair up next to the bed and leaned over his mentor.

"Alan, I need to talk to you. Are you awake, Alan?" John asked gently. He hated to wake him, but the time for getting answers seemed to be slipping away. Right along with his friend's life.

"Hummph," grunted Alan, opening one eye. He didn't say anything else, but John hoped he was awake enough.

"Alan, I need you to think back. Did Sam Denton have a key to Charlie Hanford's place back in eighty-nine? Would he have had access to the house?"

He didn't get an answer from Alan. Instead, the answer came from the other side of the room.

"Why do you want to know that?" asked Charlie from the doorway.

John could tell Charlie was trying to act casual about the question, but he sensed an edge beneath the man's relaxed facade. He matched the relaxation with a measured sigh as he stood and turned. He didn't want Charlie to feel any need to mention this to Sam.

"I'm just trying to grasp for anything and everything I can to add to the file before, well...you know," he said with a nod toward Alan. "There's virtually no evidence on the case, and one of the things I can't find in the notes is a list of who would have had access to the crime scene. It should have been pretty standard to have that list in the file with an apparent robbery, but it isn't there."

Charlie shrugged as he walked into the room. "A lot of people have access to my place. I never thought I'd have to worry about it in this town, you know?" John nodded, and Charlie went on. "Sam had a key. My housekeeper had one. Still does. Let's see... The lawn guy had a key to the garage, and from there he could get into the main part of the house. I never locked that door. Caroline had a key, of course, so she could come in to do the books."

"Did Ken Statler have a key?" John asked.

Charlie frowned. "No. No, he didn't, but wasn't the back door broken? I always thought the intruder got in that way."

John didn't answer him. He'd been looking at the pictures of the damage to the back door for years, and had always wondered if that was really the way the murderer had gotten in. The more he looked at the damage, the more he wondered if that hadn't been set up to look like the entry point when it wasn't. There were no unexpected finger-prints, nor had it been wiped clean as parts of the office had. It simply had a broken pane of glass. But, he wasn't about to share that theory with Charlie.

"Yeah, you're right. Like I said, I'm just trying to fill out the file as much as I can before Alan goes." He shrugged and stepped toward the door with a shake of his head that he hoped conveyed the message, "forget I asked," to Charlie. "It's nothing."

He could feel Charlie's eyes on him as he walked out. Any theory pointing the finger at Sam Denton, a man everyone here considered one of their own, a native born and raised in Evers, wasn't going to win John any popularity points. Luckily for him, he put his popularity, and even the issue of winning enough votes for re-election, below finding a killer on his list of priorities. He didn't care whose panties he put in a twist to catch this killer. He'd give the whole damned town wedgies if it meant finding out who killed Caroline before Katelyn was hurt and before Alan passed away.

"John!"

John spun to see Charlie standing behind him, his hands fisted in his pockets, head hanging. The older man raised his head, and John wasn't sure he'd ever seen Charlie Hanford look so unsure of himself. So hesitant.

"Yeah?" John asked.

Charlie shook his head. "I just…" Charlie glanced over his shoulder toward the door to Alan's room. "Have we been living among a killer all these years? Were we wrong about Ken Statler? Because if we were, if we've all been living with Caroline's killer all this time, it would kill him, John."

John nodded once before turning to walk away. Alan would be dying no matter what. And John honestly didn't know the answer to Charlie's question, but he had to think that knowing the truth was always a good thing. He had to believe that justice was always the right thing.

CHAPTER FOURTEEN

I f anyone had asked John to predict the following day's events, he never in a million years would have come up with this one. He shook his head as he followed Danny through the construction site that would someday be a set of apartment buildings thirty minutes outside of Evers, but still within John's county. They stepped over rebar and abandoned tools heading toward the elevator shaft. Workers had discovered Sam Denton's body at the bottom of the shaft early that morning and had called it in. It had been far too late to save Sam.

"Charlie's on his way out. He was over in Canton Falls at a project but he said he'd leave right away when I talked to him earlier. Should be here soon," Danny said over his shoulder, then stopped and hung back as though he didn't want to view the body again.

John didn't blame him. This was the worst part of their job. John took the extra few steps to the shaft and peered in.

Two sides were concrete, the other two were made up of metal joists and framework that left the cavity in the middle open. From the angle of Sam's neck, it was clear he hadn't stood a chance. He had likely died on impact. His arms and legs had suffered compound fractures, the bone in one leg protruding angrily from torn pants.

John looked up through the top of the shaft. Each floor had wooden barriers blocking the opening to the shaft except for one floor eight stories up. There, splintered remnants of a wooden barrier hung off the edge, and John could see what looked like matching pieces lying on the ground around Sam's body.

He walked back to Danny and looked at the workmen all standing outside the taped off area Danny had set when he arrived on scene ahead of John.

"Anyone know what he was doing here last night?" he asked Danny in a low voice.

"No. I asked them all what time he usually left, and they said it wasn't unusual for him to stay and work later than the rest. He may have been foreman but he didn't have any family to go home to. Sometimes, he'd just putz around a site long after everyone left, not really doing much of anything, they said." Danny looked down at his notes as he talked.

"And I take it no one was here with him?"

"Nope. Everyone else knocked off at five-thirty."

John had a hard time believing a man with as much experience as Sam Denton would have simply fallen down an elevator shaft. And it struck him as odd that the wood barrier would just give out if Sam hadn't fallen against it hard. Or been shoved against it.

He wondered about suicide. If Sam had killed Caroline, would Katelyn's return have been enough to drive him to kill himself?

But what about the broken wood? If he wanted to kill himself, wouldn't he step over the barrier?

It was possible the wood snapped when Sam tried to step over it, but something seemed off to John. He looked up to see Charlie Hanford rushing toward them from the parking lot. He looked pale and drawn as he came to a stop before them.

"Is it really Sam?" he asked, as though he were still holding out hope that Danny might have been wrong.

"Charlie," said John, holding his hands out to stop Charlie's progress toward the body, "I'm sorry. It looks like it happened sometime last night after everyone left." The coroner's van pulled up as John spoke. "We'll know more after the coroner issues her report."

Charlie stared past John at the spot where Sam lay as the coroner picked her way through the obstacle course leading to the body.

"I should have pulled him off the job," he said, his voice heavily laden with regret.

"Why do you say that?" John asked, studying the man's body language as he waited for an answer. The hair on John's neck stood on end, a signal he'd learned to heed a long time ago. Listening had saved his life more than once in his line of work. He seemed to get that feeling around

Charlie a lot, but he couldn't pinpoint a reason. Maybe he'd just picked up on Katelyn's hesitation about the man, given her feelings toward her father's best friend.

Charlie pulled his eyes off the elevator shaft and focused on John. "He was having trouble lately. He'd forget things. I'd find him on a site, disoriented. One night, I came back to pick something up I'd forgotten and he was there. It was midnight, and he was walking around in his boxer shorts. I started talking to him and it was like he thought he was in his own house. He brushed it off, tried to joke about it, told me he'd just had a little too much to drink after everyone went home. The next day he was fine, and I didn't see any signs of any problems as serious as that again. I... Oh hell, I didn't have the heart to take him off the job. I had him doing less and less. Just supervising, but not working hands-on with anything."

"It's all right, Charlie," John said, but in his head he wondered what Charlie thought would happen if he let someone showing signs of dementia work on a construction site. And John had seen Sam working pretty hands-on only last week at Katelyn's studio. He'd been hanging drywall and installing lights.

It took Danny and John about ten more minutes to console Charlie before John was able to get a minute alone with the coroner and Danny. John and Danny climbed down into the elevator shaft, joining Dr. Catherine Tanner, the county coroner who was also the medical examiner. The dual role was a blessing for the county. Not such a blessing for Cathy, who was paid one salary for fulfilling both sets of duties. John never understood why she hadn't put her medical training to use doing something that would have earned her more money, but she seemed to be content staying where she was.

"What can you tell me so far, Cathy?"

She pulled off her soiled gloves as she spoke. "Time of death was approximately eight p.m. to midnight last night. Cause of death is clear. Broken neck. I suspect the trauma to his spinal cord would have been significant enough to cause immediate spinal shock and a very quick death, but I can't confirm that until I do the autopsy, if you want one."

John glanced around and then nodded. He couldn't shake the feeling that something was wrong. Sam Denton had grown up on construction sites with his father. He'd been foreman for at least twenty-five years. It seemed as if avoiding an accident like this would be second nature to him. And, John wasn't willing to believe this was a coincidence. Any connection he'd begun to make between Sam Denton and Caroline Bowden's murder was a loose one—hell, it was full of holes—but something told him there was a whole lot more going on here than a construction site accident.

"Let's do a full autopsy. Also, run a tox screen. I want to know why he went through those boards up there. It's possible this was an accident. Charlie Hanford described some behavior...episodes that might explain him going through them on his own. That's most likely what happened, but let's check and recheck everything so we can be sure about that before we sign off on this one."

John angled his body away from the crowd of onlookers, making sure only Danny and the coroner could hear him. "We're going to treat this as a suspicious death, but I want that information kept quiet for now. I don't want anyone to know we think this is more than just an accident."

If the crime scene had anything to do with Caroline Bowden's murderer, John wanted to be sure they didn't chase the killer right back into hiding. May Bishop was right. The more active this killer became, the more likely a screw-up was going to happen. And John planned to be there when this killer made a mistake.

"You got it," Cathy said, her trademark commitment to thoroughness no doubt making it easy for her to agree. "Labs'll take a week or more. I'll keep you posted."

"What do you want me to do, boss?" Danny asked.

Danny's eager, young-pup demeanor would come in handy here. "Check on the pieces of wood down here and up above to be sure there aren't any signs they've been tampered with. And I want you to continue to ask all the guys working under Sam about his behavior lately. See if they saw anything like Charlie described. But let them think you're just checking off the routine boxes on an accident investigation. Heck, for all we know, that's what this is. If you have to, gripe about me making you do busy work. Just be sure no one thinks this is us trying to take this to a higher level, got it?"

"You got it, boss."

KATELYN WALKED into the kitchen just as John was starting the coffee brewing. As she reached into the cabinet to pull down two mugs, his arms came around her from behind, pulling her in to him and immediately setting her body ablaze. John seemed to be taking things slow with her, not pushing her to have sex yet, and she appreciated that. His sleeping on the couch could have too easily turned into an excuse for them to jump right into more. That didn't mean his simple act of holding her didn't start an ache racing through her body, an ache that was getting harder to ignore.

"I love waking up to find you here with me," he said, nuzzling the side of her face and neck with his mouth.

Katelyn laughed. "It's my kitchen. Where else would you find me?"

"Oh yeah." He pulled back and turned her so she faced him, then caged her against the counter with his arms.

Katelyn smiled. "I like waking up to find you here," she said, her hands running over his chest. He slept on the couch every night, despite the fact that it was likely the most uncomfortable contraption ever made and at least four inches too short for him. But his consideration was nice.

Really nice. He was as turned on by her as she was by him—he couldn't actually hide that—but she didn't feel any pressure to have sex with him yet. He was incredibly different from Devan in that way. Devan's whole motivation, as it turned out, was sex. Apparently, with a newborn at home, he'd decided to go elsewhere and she'd been the elsewhere.

With John, she knew it wasn't just about getting in her pants. Or her bed.

"What are you smiling at?" John asked, breaking into her thoughts.

Katelyn shook her head. "Just happy, that's all."

John released her with a grin as he reached around her for the now-full coffee pot and filled their cups.

"Hey, how did things go with that boy? That one you're trying to help? Did he come in to talk to you like you asked or was he a no-show again?" she asked.

"Trent? He checked himself into rehab. I've got a couple of people in town who said they'd give him a job when he gets out, and he seemed pretty motivated to make it through. He's got thirty days in there and then we'll see what happens." He shrugged as though he didn't care, but she knew he did. A lot.

"You did a good thing."

He grunted. "Maybe. We'll see if it makes a difference. I can't turn my back on it again if I catch him drinking. He's underage. Luckily for him, a lot of people in this town want to see him get out from under his dad's thumb and make it. He's got people willing to help him."

"I have a feeling they're willing to help you and by extension they'll help him. It's the fact that you're going out on a limb to help him that's making the difference," Katelyn said.

She saw a tiny telltale pink tinge beneath John's tan and decided she'd let him off the hook. She changed the subject. "Do you like running?"

"Hate it," he said. "It's my least favorite form of exercise. Why?"

Katelyn frowned. "Oh. Never mind."

John gave her his look again and pulled her into his arms, tipping her chin up so she had no choice but to look at him.

"Why, Kate?"

"Katelyn." She said into his chest, burying her head again. She loved the smell of him.

"Why?"

"I wanted you to run with me. I don't want to go alone."

"I said I hate running, not that I don't do it. It's sort of a requirement when you're a cop. Gotta keep in shape. Besides, I won't mind running with you," he said as his mouth began to trail over her shoulder, sending heat and shivers through her in a delicious combination.

"Why?" she asked, hearing the way her breath caught as his mouth ran up her neck and he explored the soft spot behind her ear. Her heart sped up and her mind began to wander to her bedroom. Maybe—

"Because I'll just stay behind you. I have a feeling I'm gonna love running behind you, Katelyn," he said, drawing her name out with the sexy huskiness that told her he was as affected by what he was doing as she was. One strong hand traveled down to cup her backside.

All thoughts of running and exercise and fear of leaving the house alone left her brain, just skittered right out of her head as John and his kisses took over.

CHAPTER FIFTEEN

J ohn kept Katelyn close to him over the next few days. If he wasn't with her, one of his men was. She visited her father in the hospital every day despite the fact he had more and more days when he wasn't coherent. John could see Alan was slipping away from them. He and Katelyn both wanted to bring Alan home, but John was worried about having him at the house. It seemed safer to leave him at the hospital where he was surrounded by staff 24/7.

With Sam Denton's death, construction on Katelyn's studio slowed for a few days, but Charlie promised he'd have a new foreman in place by the end of the week. Rumors about Sam's strange behavior seemed to surface overnight and filled conversations in the Two Sisters' booths. What bothered John most was that no one had mentioned any of this before his death, and all of the stories sounded like a reiteration of the ones Charlie had told John.

John was willing to bet if he dug hard enough, he'd find all of those stories led back to one source.

All of these things ate at the back of John's mind as he followed the long dirt road out to Holland Barnett's farm and took the cutoff he knew would take him around back to the old barn and pond. Holland didn't farm his land anymore, and he hadn't had any children to take it over. He'd sold off some parcels of the once-large property to surrounding farms, but kept the land that held his barn and house.

John had a vague memory of hearing that the county's search and rescue team ran drills on Holland's land, but he hadn't expected to get a call from them like the one he'd had this morning. He parked his cruiser behind one of the search and rescue trucks and got out. Adam Dean greeted him almost immediately, while the rest of the search team stayed back with their dogs either sitting by their sides or in dog crates in the back of SUVs parked around Holland's old barn.

"Hey, Adam," John said, shaking the search team leader's hand. "Tell me again what you told Berta. She was all up in arms about dead bodies in Holland's pond."

"Well," Adam said, rubbing the back of his neck as he spoke, "she's probably overreacting. Heck, we all probably are, but I figured I should call it in."

"Okay," John said slowly, looking at the rest of the team then back to Adam.

"We usually use this location to work our live find dogs, but this morning we were running our newer cadaver dogs out here. They're trained to detect human remains," Adam said.

John nodded. He was familiar with search and rescue dogs. A live find dog is trained to find any live human in a given area. Cadaver dogs were just the opposite. They alerted on any human remains—tissue, blood, placental or fetal tissue, teeth, bone. They'd occasionally used cadaver dogs for finding evidence like a blood trail when he was a cop in New York City.

"We weren't working the pond, but one of the dogs went off in that direction on her own and we didn't stop her. She gave an alert on the water."

That was new to John.

"They can do that? Smell human remains under water?" he asked. He knew they were good, but that seemed miraculous.

"Sometimes, especially with such a small body of water. If there are human remains in the water, the vegetation all around the pond will have the scent of the remains growing right in them. We don't start cadaver dogs out with anything as complicated as a water find, but when our dogs get more experienced, we work them on water. She's a green dog so she wasn't working water yet and the alert was weak. But, I brought another dog over to the area to have them run it just out of curiosity." Adam looked almost apologetic as he spoke, and John had a bad feeling about what this was leading up to.

"And?" He was almost afraid to ask. He could see Holland walking toward them from the house, and the last thing he wanted to deal with was telling Holland Barnett they had reason to believe there was a dead body on his property.

"He alerted also. I called in two of our experienced cadaver dogs to check it before calling you. All four dogs have alerted on the pond."

Before John could respond, Holland joined them, seemingly unconcerned that John was there.

"Hey, John, I was fixin' to come out and get you earlier in the week, but I hadn't gotten around to it," Holland said, holding a key out to John, apparently thinking nothing of the fact that John was out there. John quickly eliminated Holland off any mental suspect list. The man wouldn't have let the search team or anyone else run around on his property if he'd known there was a body in the pond.

John looked down at the key Holland had put in his hand. "What's this?" he asked.

Holland jerked his head toward the barn. "Key to the barn. Sam Denton rented it from me for the last twenty-five years."

John frowned. He hadn't realized it had been that long since Holland had farmed this land, but it made sense. The man was well into his eighties, and he'd been injured in an accident sometime before John had moved to Evers. He got around surprisingly well, but farming would have been more than he could do.

"He used it for storage and such. I don't know what all he kept in there, but seeing as he had no kin around here, I thought I should give the key to you."

"Thanks. I'll have to deal with that another day," John said, wondering what he'd do with Sam Denton's junk. Sam's landlord had cleaned out Sam's small apartment after John and Conner had gone through it.

"We have a bit of a sensitive issue with your pond. Seems the cadaver dogs have alerted on it. Can I send a diver in there to take a look, see what they might be alerting on?"

Holland looked at him like John couldn't pour water out of a boot if the instructions were written on the heel. "There's all kinds of dead animals in that pond, I'm sure."

Adam shook his head. "They're trained not to alert on any dead tissue that's not human. The first two dogs that alerted are green so they might still make that mistake, especially with the find under water, but not the two seasoned dogs we brought in. There's something in there."

Holland looked at Adam and back to John, then back to Adam before he started to laugh. It was a chuffing, breathless sort of laugh that made John wonder if they'd need to call in paramedics to give him oxygen before all this was over. Holland never did really recover the ability to speak. He just waved his hand and nodded, then walked in the house, almost bent over with laughter at the two of them.

"Guess that's permission to search," John said and keyed his radio.

"Berta, call Dale Byer. See if he can come dive this pond for me and take a look. And see if Danny and Carter are free. Send them out here, too."

The radio crackled with her reply and John and Adam

sat down to wait. They tried to send the rest of the search team home, but no one was budging, and John knew it wasn't worth the effort to try to make them. They'd most likely already texted the rest of the town to come out and watch the show, too.

Sure enough, cars started creeping up the drive soon after, and Danny and Carter were put to work keeping people away from a possible crime scene instead of doing any real work for John. He watched and waited as Dale suited up to go under and take a look. Chances were he wouldn't find anything. John hoped he wouldn't, anyway.

He had his answer soon after when Dale surfaced and pulled off his mask. He was pale as a ghost when he waded out and walked up to them. John swallowed a curse.

Dale huddled close to Adam and John before speaking. "There's a truck down there." He looked at John almost as if he wished he weren't about to say what he was, as much as John wished he wasn't about to hear it. "There's a body in the front. Well, not a body. Bones. Nothing left but bones on the seat and floorboards of the cab. Whole truck's rotted and covered in grime like it's been in there a long time, John. I've only ever seen anything like it on TV."

The look on Dale's face told John he wasn't joking. He keyed his radio once again. "Berta, send Catherine out to Holland's and get me a tow truck."

"Holy crap," was her initial response followed by a, "yes, boss."

John rolled his eyes. *A circus. This was going to be an absolute freaking circus.*

And that's what it was over the next two hours while the truck was pulled up out of the water. Dale kept his cool long enough to help get the tow truck hooked up underwater. Holland came back out around the time the truck was being pulled up. How he recognized the relic, John would never know, but he immediately spotted it as Ken Statler's truck, the missing construction worker suspected of killing Katelyn's mother. The truck that had supposedly been in Charlie Hanford's driveway the day of Caroline's murder. John wondered if the truck had gone into the water before or after Caroline was killed.

"And what do you want to bet, those are Ken Statler's bones in there?" John muttered under his breath. He turned and looked at the old barn standing twenty yards from the pond. *That's no coincidence.*

"Danny!" John called out to his deputy, who left the line of gawkers to jog toward John.

"Yeah, boss?"

John slipped the barn key out of his pocket and handed it to Danny. "Holland has given permission to search the barn. We'll need to call in everyone we can to work this scene, too. We're looking for anything connected to Ken Statler or—"

"Holy—" Danny cut in but stopped himself, looking at John. "Ken Statler, as in the suspect in Caroline Bowden's murder—*that* Ken Statler?"

John nodded grimly. "Yeah. Look for anything connected to him or to Caroline Bowden. It looks like we might solve this for Alan after all."

CHAPTER SIXTEEN

John quietly let himself into Katelyn's house hours later. He expected her to be upstairs in bed, but she was curled up on the couch asleep. Maybe that meant she hadn't gotten any calls or texts yet about the find out at Holland's place. He didn't know how he'd tell her all they'd found that night, but he knew one thing, he wasn't planning to tell her until the morning.

He looked down at Kate sleeping and knew he was starting to feel things for her he hadn't felt in a very long time. If ever, really. He had thought he loved Lexi, but now, years after her death, he knew it wasn't true. Heck, he probably knew it at the time. He just didn't want to face it.

Being so far undercover for so long was isolating. You had to give up all your instincts to protect, give up all that you were as a cop. He didn't know how many times he'd watched a crime take place and not called it in, even anonymously, because he had to keep the big picture in mind. If anyone put two-and-two together and figured out he'd been the one to report something, he was done. Getting Eddie off the streets had taken priority. He'd turned away from a robbery in progress once because he couldn't blow his cover. He'd had to choose between trying to convince the women in the gang to get out—to get themselves away and get help, instead of living a life where they were constantly subjected to abuse and rape and unimaginable violence—and maintaining his cover. It had sickened him every time he'd been faced with that choice.

In that setting, he'd clung to Lexi as an anchor. It hadn't been fair to her, but he'd done it nonetheless, knowing he needed something—someone—to keep him sane.

What he felt for Katelyn was nothing like what he'd felt for Lexi. He was with Kate for all the right reasons. What he felt for her was so deep and real, it scared him sometimes. But, it also felt right in a way he'd never experienced before.

John lifted Katelyn and started up the stairs to her room. She turned and snuggled into his chest, burrowing closer as she slipped her arms around him.

Yup. It just felt right.

"Wha ha oo ow so ate?" she said into his chest bringing a smile to his face. Katelyn was not very articulate in her sleep. She also must be the only person in town who hadn't heard about their find out at Holland's place and for that he was grateful. He'd tell her everything tomorrow. Then they'd go over and tell her father what they'd found.

Katelyn raised her head and tried again. "What had you out so late?"

He didn't answer her question. John looked at her mussed up hair, tired eyes, and the red marks from where her cheek had pressed into the fabric of the couch, and he was lost. Who was he kidding? He probably wouldn't make it another night without peeling off her clothes and losing himself in the soft curves of her body, in the heat that burned with every touch of their skin. Sure, if she stopped him, he'd find a way. It would probably involve an extremely long, very cold shower and returning to the couch, but he hoped she wanted to be with him as much as he wanted to be with her.

John set her down in her bed and lowered himself over her, watching the small gasp and the way her eyes lit up. He lowered his head to her collarbone and let his tongue sweep the soft curve of it, relishing in the shiver that ran through her body in response. As his mouth trailed over her shoulder and up to the soft skin just behind her ears, she wriggled closer still, pressing the full length of her body against his. From her sighs and moans, she didn't have any interest in him moving back to the couch, either.

John groaned as her body pressed against the hard length of his erection. He half wondered if he was dreaming when she whispered in his ear asking him to make love to her. But, when he pulled back and looked in her eyes, he knew it wasn't a dream. And, he knew he was powerless to refuse her.

John pulled the T-shirt and shorts from her body and

looked down at her. She was so beautiful. So incredible lying there for him, her skin creamy and silky smooth. He wanted to lick and nibble every part of her, to find out what would make her whimper, how he could make her scream.

"Heaven," he whispered as his mouth took hers again and he let his hands explore her eager body. She responded to him in a way no woman ever had, arching into his hands, his mouth, as if she couldn't get enough.

John stood and undressed, never taking his eyes from her flushed face. His cock sprang from his boxers, seeming to strain toward her as if by reaching for her it could make this happen faster. But, John didn't want fast.

He slipped her panties from her body and slid her bra down her arms, revealing peaked nipples. John shoved aside the urge to bury himself balls deep in her and found one nipple with his mouth, the other with his hand. Her responding moan was all the encouragement he needed to slide a hand between her legs. She was wet and swollen, her lips parting for his fingers as she slid her legs further apart in welcome.

"John, please," she whispered, almost snapping his control. As his hands moved over her clit and his teeth tugged at one breast, before moving to her neck and the spot behind her ear that seemed to send her back to arching anytime he neared it. John gritted his teeth to hold out. He wanted to see her come, to hear her come.

When she shattered under him, he watched in awe. Her face was a mask of ecstasy, of pleasure so great, he knew he wanted to give her that again and again.

John grabbed a condom package from his pocket and tore it open with his teeth. He covered himself before resting the head of his erection at her entrance and looking into her eyes. She whimpered as she wrapped her arms around his neck and pulled him closer, pushing up with straining hips. John sank into her inch by inch, reveling in the feel of the tight heat that welcomed him.

The groan that escaped his chest was visceral, a response to sheer and utter pleasure. A sensation so overwhelming, he almost lost control as his hips began to rock, plunging his cock deeper into her tight heat. She rose to meet him with each stroke and raked her hands up his back, the slight sharpness of her nails nearly sending him over the edge.

John shifted her beneath him, grasping her hips and pinning her to the bed as he increased his pace, knowing she was moments from another orgasm and hoping he could hold out as the slick walls of her vagina began to quiver and pulse around him.

"Katelyn," he said on a moan, a plea, as he felt her orgasm race through her and he joined her this time, giving in to the snap at the base of his balls. His body emptied, completely draining him as his head fell to her shoulder.

He had made love to her with a passion and intensity he'd never felt, and she reciprocated just as fiercely. John lost himself in Katelyn, lost himself to the sensations and emotions of being with a woman he now knew he loved. There was no more denying what he felt for her.

KATELYN LAY in John's arms hoping and praying that being with him meant as much to him as it had to her. Because as soon as she'd whispered in his ear, she'd realized it was going to mean everything to her to make love to this man. He had quickly become her everything. And the thought that maybe he wasn't headed in the same direction with this relationship scared the daylights out of her.

She hadn't thought she would ever feel this way for a man, especially so quickly after Devan's betrayal. If she had to give John up now, it would kill her.

His arms played up and down her back, warming and sending shivers through her at the same time. He pulled the sheet up over her shoulders, but then let his hands continue to rub as she nuzzled down into the bed, not wanting to think about what-if and what-happens-when anymore.

"Kate," John said, but it was more of a question than the start of a statement, and Katelyn stilled. Whenever he called her "Kate" he always seemed to be trying to soften the blow of something.

Oh, no. No, don't...This didn't mean anything to him.

Katelyn sat up, pulling the covers around herself. She looked down at John, half wanting to run away before he could reject her, but part of her still hoping she was wrong. A very small, quiet, simpering-in-the-corner part of her.

John reached up and pushed the hair out of her eyes, tucking errant strands behind one ear.

Say it. Katelyn braced herself.

"We found something today," he started, his hand running down her arm as he spoke.

What?

Katelyn blinked, not sure what he was talking about, but sure the conversation wasn't the one she'd thought it would be. "What?"

"I wasn't going to tell you until the morning." She watched him, waiting for him to tell her what he clearly didn't want to spit out. "I think we may have found your mother's killer."

Katelyn felt the air leave her all at once. She let herself fall back down into John's arms. They came around her, holding her tight as he explained about the dogs and the pond, the rotted-out truck and decomposed body.

John's voice was quiet and steady as he told her everything. "When your mom was murdered, there was a stone bookend that went missing from Charlie Hanford's office. We have the matching one of the set in evidence, and we've always believed the missing one was the murder weapon." Katelyn held tightly to John as he told her they'd found the matching bookend in the truck they suspected was Ken Statler's.

She took a deep breath, trying to figure out how she felt about the news. She honestly didn't know. Mostly, she felt the urge to go tell her father. He deserved to know after all this time.

"I don't understand, though. If he killed my mom, who killed him?"

"Well," John blew out a breath and seemed to brace

himself to deliver the rest of the story, "we think it might have been Sam Denton."

"What? Why? Why would Sam do that?" Katelyn sat up and looked at John. How could someone who'd lived in their town, saw her father all the time, someone so close to her father's best friend—how could he have had anything to do with her mother's murder? "Why would he do that?" She asked again, trying to wrap her mind around what he was telling her.

"I don't know, hon. I probably shouldn't even tell you all of this until we really have answers, but since Sam and Ken are both dead, and the evidence is completely compromised from being underwater for so long, it's entirely possible we won't get any concrete answers. I can only tell you what I think happened."

Katelyn looked down, playing with the hair that fell down around her shoulders, wondering for a minute how much she wanted to know. When she looked back up, John was watching her, waiting patiently.

"What do you think happened?" she asked, almost hating how small her own voice sounded. She wanted to be stronger than this.

"I began to suspect Sam a few days ago. He was just too involved in every aspect of your mom's case and in the attack on you. He seemed to be the one pointing the finger at Ken Statler all these years. Sam Denton leased the barn next to the pond on Holland's property. We got a warrant. When we opened the barn after we found the truck, we discovered tools and things belonging to Ken Statler in the barn."

Katelyn could practically feel her eyebrows knitting together in confusion, and John must have seen it too. "I don't get it myself, but a bunch of the guys at the scene today have worked construction. They assured me it would have been tough for a guy like Sam who'd been in construction all his life to toss those tools. They were a really nice set, very expensive stuff. Seems Ken didn't stay in one place very long or have a fancy home, but he took pride in his trade. Bought the best carpentry tools he could afford."

John shrugged a shoulder. "I guess Sam couldn't bring himself to get rid of them, but he also couldn't use them on the job. There are too many guys who work for Charlie that were working for him when Statler was around, and who would have recognized the initials carved in them. Best I can tell, either Sam or Ken killed your mother. Maybe they went to steal the petty cash from Charlie together and they surprised your mom. For whatever reason, Sam must have killed Ken after that. Maybe he wanted to keep him quiet. Maybe he thought it would be a good idea to make it look like Ken had left town after your mother's murder. It's possible Ken killed your mother and then Sam killed him out of revenge? He might have had a crush on your mom—who knows? I don't think we ever will. But I'm fairly sure one of them killed your mother and then Sam killed Ken."

"But, we won't ever really know for sure," Katelyn said. It was more of a statement than a question as she tried to process what John had just told her. It felt a little better knowing whoever had killed her mother was no longer out there. Although, if it had been Sam and he'd been able to live a full life while her mother had missed out on so much hurt a lot. Knowing it was someone so close to home hurt even more.

Katelyn let out a long slow breath. "So that's it? It's over?"

John nodded. "I think so. When we went through Sam's apartment, I found some clothes that looked like they may have blood on them. I'm having them checked to see if it's blood. If it is, we'll run it to see if it's yours from the night of the attack." John brushed his lips over her temple as he spoke and held her close. "See if his truck has any evidence that it was him who ran you off the road that night you were jogging."

"Oh God. I hadn't even thought of that," Katelyn said, bile rushing up her throat. "I saw him almost every day over at the studio when I went by to check on things. How could he look me in the eye every day and then attack me like that?"

"I don't know, baby. But, he had us all fooled. He sat on your dad's couch watching the game with us dozens of times. I honestly don't know how he did it. It's very possible his death was a suicide. We haven't found a note anywhere, but it could be that having you back here set him off. The coroner is looking into it right now. She'll know more soon, and I'll re-interview people now that we have new information. See if anything else turns up."

John sounded bitter and angry and she knew he was

thinking of her father. "Try to get some sleep, hon, and we'll go tell your dad in the morning," John said with one last kiss.

Katelyn closed her eyes, but she didn't try to sleep. Her mind wouldn't stop spinning. Her emotions were on overload. Making love to John had been everything she'd ever hoped for and more. Things just felt so natural, so right with him. In that way, her heart was so full. But she also couldn't keep her thoughts from her mother's death and her father's life-long quest to find the truth.

She lay for what felt like hours in John's arms, and she knew he wasn't sleeping either, but neither of them seemed to feel the need to speak. There wasn't really anything she could say. She hadn't been close to Sam, but he was a part of her father's world all this time. What did you say to the news of such betrayal when someone you'd known your whole life had been the one to take your mother from you? To news you'd waited for all your life, but now almost wished you didn't have. Maybe it would have been better for her father not to know who had done this to him, who had taken away the woman he loved.

CHAPTER SEVENTEEN

Katelyn must have slept because she woke in John's arms. He didn't look like he'd slept at all. In fact, she could all but see his mind working, and she knew he must have spent the whole night working through what needed to be done to wrap up her mother's case, to the extent a case could be wrapped up where all of the suspects were already dead.

"Did you sleep?" she asked, pulling back to look him in the eyes, then quickly missing the warmth and security of his arms. She always felt safe when he wrapped her up in him like she was some tiny treasure he'd protect at all costs. Katelyn took a deep breath and realized she didn't need to worry about that anymore. Sam Denton was dead. She *was* safe now.

"A little bit," he said.

He nuzzled into her neck, but she knew he was lying. She couldn't help but arch her back and sigh when his lips traveled over her shoulders. It was incredible what he managed to do to her body with only the whisper of his mouth on her shoulders, of all things.

And he did more incredible things with his mouth as he pulled the sheets back and rolled her beneath him, all the while never losing contact. Katelyn let herself get lost in the feel of his body pressed against hers, in the heat and emotion of the moment as he made love to her sweetly, quietly, as though he never wanted the moment to end. As though he wanted to bind them together forever.

If it were any other day, they would have likely stayed in bed. But they needed to see her father—to tell him about Ken and Sam. They didn't speak when they got up and showered together an hour later, but the quiet was comfortable. It was as if they both knew that the morning would be a hard one, telling her father something he'd waited more than twenty years to hear, but both knowing there wouldn't be much comfort in the knowledge for him. Knowing the knowledge had come too late for him, much too late for justice.

John handed a glass of orange juice to Katelyn and poured another for himself as she popped bread in the toaster and grabbed peanut butter from the pantry. John sliced bananas to go on top of his. Katelyn thought it was gross, but he just laughed when she told him that. He said it was the perfect combination of sweet and salty with the peanut butter, and the right combination of dry and mushy with the toast and the banana.

"You're slow," John said with a laugh as he pulled

Katelyn into his lap while she finished her toast. He'd swallowed his two pieces in what seemed like four bites apiece, and watched as she finished her first piece and picked up her second.

"No," Katelyn said, smiling. "I just don't eat like a caveman. Besides," she said, losing her smile, "I really don't want to do this. I thought it'd be great to find out who killed my mom. I thought it would be a relief to tell my dad, but it's not. I think it's going to hurt him more than help him at this point."

"Are you sure you want to tell him? He probably won't be with us much longer. Maybe it's better for him not to know."

She just looked at him, and he nodded. "Yeah, you're right. We have to tell him," he said.

JOHN WAS CRUSHED by the look of shock on Alan's face when they told him what they'd found at Holland's farm. Telling him what they thought Sam had done was even harder than John had imagined it would be, and that told him he was just too damned close to the situation. Charlie was at the hospital when they arrived, so he stayed with Alan while they broke the news, and looked every bit as shocked as Alan. He kept apologizing for bringing Sam into Alan's life, even though no one could blame him for that. Sam and Alan had both been born and raised in Evers.

Sam's misdeeds weren't Charlie's fault, and the fact that he worked for Charlie didn't change that.

Katelyn was quiet through most of it, holding her father's hand. She looked as relieved as John felt when her father closed his eyes and let the pain medication lull him to sleep soon after they'd told him. He was awake less and less these days and John was sure the sleep was a blessing right now. He didn't look remotely like the man John had come to think of as a father. His face was swollen almost beyond recognition most days as his liver failed to do the job it was meant to do.

His legs were so swollen he couldn't get out of bed any longer. The doctors told Katelyn and John it was a matter of days at this point before he would go, and seeing him so broken, so broke down, hurt like hell.

John looked up at Kate and saw tears streaming silently down her face. He walked around the bed to her and stood behind her, holding her tightly as she watched her father. Charlie nodded and slipped out of the room, and John knew he and Katelyn had just started their death watch over her father. He had already told Berta not to call him in for anything that wasn't an absolute emergency. Danny would take over for the next week while John and Kate sat with Alan.

"You know he loved you so much? He used to tell me about your art, about his amazingly talented daughter. He said you got that from your mom. He always told me she should have been an artist like you instead of a bookkeeper.

He was proud of you for following your dream, living your passion."

Katelyn nodded and sniffled and John went on, telling her about the way her father bragged about her when she graduated from college or the way he couldn't stop talking about her first showing at a gallery.

"He won't get to see his grandchildren," she said quietly, and John's heart ached for her.

"Do you want to have children?" he whispered, hearing the catch in his own voice as his emotions took over.

She nodded.

"We'll have as many as you want," he whispered and realized he meant every word of it. He hadn't recognized it but somewhere along the way, he had realized he'd spend his life with Katelyn. He'd marry her and build a family and a home and a life with her. "As many as you want, Katelyn."

She nodded again, and he felt tears splash on his forearm.

John pulled her back to the armchair in the corner and sat down, drawing her into his lap. They stayed that way as the doctors and nurses came and went. They got up occasionally throughout the night and the following day for bathroom breaks or to eat a bit here or there, but neither was very hungry.

Alan began to have what almost looked like seizures, his legs moving uncontrollably, and Katelyn sobbed in John's arms while the nurses increased the morphine drip. Alan's body stilled the following morning and Katelyn's sobs quieted again.

Alan didn't wake up again. Their last conversation had been the news about Sam Denton. He died thirty-two hours later. It was almost as though he'd waited. Waited for his wife's killer all those years. John took Katelyn home and tucked her into bed then slid in next to her and held her while she slept. The tears finally stopped. At least for a while.

CHAPTER EIGHTEEN

Katelyn watched as the casserole brigade, led by Mrs. J., swarmed into the house after the funeral. It was funny to think that just a couple of months ago she'd resented these people and this town. She'd felt like an outsider and hated the way they looked at her. Now, as Laura and Ashley and Cora surrounded her on the couch in her father's living room, and the people of the town brought her enough food to last for the next five years, she felt she'd finally come home. At last.

"He was a hell of a guy, your dad, Kit Kat," Ashley said as she slipped a cup of hot coffee into Katelyn's hands. Katelyn actually laughed at the nickname for once. It seemed as though it was going to stick. Ashley didn't seem likely to be giving it up anytime soon.

"You would know, Ash. You did know him better than any of us," Cora said wryly and Katelyn looked at her quizzically. Cora smiled with a tinge of sadness. "Your dad was always bringing Ashley home from one mess or another she'd gotten herself into."

Ashley made a show of primping her skirt until it lay just right across her lap as Laura and Katelyn looked at her, awaiting a response. Neither of the women had grown up in Evers, so any stories about Ashley as a teen were new to them both.

"What?" She shrugged a shoulder and shook her head. "I was just livelier than Cora was, that's all."

Cora let out an inelegant snort. "Livelier. Sure." She turned to Katelyn. "Your dad had to drive her home whenever she snuck out after bedtime. Oh, and then there was that time she tried to climb the water tower to write her and Jimmy Kendall's initials on the side of it, but she froze halfway up the ladder."

Cora sounded like she could hardly catch her breath for the laughter coming from her. "She actually had to flag down Haddie Gilman and have her call your dad that time and ask him to come get her down!"

Laura and Katelyn laughed while Ashley tried to look offended but failed. She gave in and grinned at them, and Katelyn was relieved for the break in the sadness of the day.

"Enough stories about me, Cora Bora," Ashley said, with a childish scowl in her sister's direction.

"Cora Bora?" Laura and Katelyn echoed at once.

Ashley's answering grin was devilish and Cora rolled her eyes.

"My name for Cora when we were younger," Ashley said.

"Because I was sooooo boring."

When the laughter died down, John caught Katelyn's eye across the room and smiled at her. He stood speaking with several of the men that had served with his father throughout the years.

"His eulogy was beautiful," Laura said, nodding at John. She was right. It had been.

He'd talked about the way he'd been a broken man when he came to town. How her father had somehow managed to show him that life was worth living, that he had something he could still give to people. He talked about what her father had meant to the county and the people he served. What he'd meant to his officers and the people he'd mentored. What he meant to his friends. He talked about her father's love for her mother, and how he'd loved her until the day he died.

Katelyn knew people were beginning to whisper about her mother's murder and what had been discovered about Sam and Ken, but she didn't care. Not today. Today, she just wanted to let her friends surround her with laughter. She wanted to eat casseroles that were too rich and much too high in calories. She wanted to hear stories about her father and what he meant to people. She'd deal with the fallout of Sam Denton and the resolution to a mystery that was decades old tomorrow.

It was late in the evening by the time Mrs. J. and her casserole brigade had packed all of the leftovers into the fridge and shooed most of the guests out the door after Katelyn thanked them for coming.

"Why don't we do a girls' night out tomorrow?" Laura asked as she hugged Katelyn goodbye.

"I'm in," Ashley said and Cora nodded.

"Margaritas at my place?" Cora said looking at Katelyn for confirmation.

"Sounds perfect. I can bring some of the leftover food. If I don't get some of it out of the house, I'll be twenty pounds heavier by next week," Katelyn said.

John walked up to the group and slipped his arms around Katelyn's waist. No one seemed surprised by the move, and she guessed the Evers grapevine had already spread the news they were seeing each other.

"You've lost weight and you didn't really have any room to lose it, Kate," John said with a frown.

Ashley leaned forward, not even remotely trying to keep her stage-whispered words quiet. "Somebody's trying to get laid tonight."

Katelyn would have laughed but before she knew what was happening, Mrs. J. was there with her purse bashing poor John over the head with it and chasing him out of the house behind all of the other guests. She kept saying something about "God-fearing men waited" and "not in her town." Katelyn stood shell-shocked as John's cruiser pulled away from the house and she was left with Mrs. J. ushering her up the stairs to her room.

She sat on the edge of the bed and looked at her phone. Would it be needy to call and ask him to come back? He was probably tired of running home for clean clothes every morning and living his life without any of his things around.

Maybe now that her father was gone and the threat to her seemed to be over, it was time things went back to normal. Time he went home. Katelyn eyed the phone and debated.

Clack, clack, clack.

She swung around at the sound of stones hitting her bedroom window. Even as her head told her it couldn't be John, her heart flipped in her chest. *Please be John. Please be John.*

Katelyn shoved the window up, the old, stiff tracks making it hard to get up more than half way. She stuck her head out and laughed at the sight of the county's sheriff whispering and watching over his head for any sign of Mrs. J.

"Open the back door," John whispered up at her, and Katelyn had to stifle a laugh as she pushed the window closed and ran to the stairs. She felt like a teenager sneaking around, but didn't care. He was here. He'd come back before she'd even had a chance to call him.

"Where'd you leave your car?" she asked as John pushed in and lifted her off the floor with one arm around her waist and the other shoving the door shut. He didn't answer. His mouth was busy laying a track of heat and hunger down the side of her neck. He traced his way across her collar bone and her body responded instantly, heating and aching with need.

He walked to the kitchen table and set Katelyn down on it, never breaking contact with her skin. His mouth moved back to capture hers, engulfing her and wiping away memories and pain. She wrapped her arms around his neck and sank into him, reveling in the feel of his strong arm around her, his mouth hot and needy on hers, letting her know he needed this as much as she did. After a kiss that turned her mind to nothing more than mush, John broke away long enough to answer her question, making her wish she'd never asked.

"I parked around the corner and snuck through the backyards."

Katelyn couldn't stop the laugh this time. All she could picture was a neighbor calling the police, and one of John's own deputies showing up to catch him in the act of sneaking into her house. "Maybe we should move upstairs so no one spots us and calls the police."

"Or worse, Mrs. J.," John said, wrapping her legs around his waist as he lifted her.

The feel of his muscles cradled in the heat between her legs, heat he'd created, only ignited her body all the more.

Katelyn didn't spare a second thought for Mrs. J. after that. John didn't let her. His assault on her senses was all-encompassing and overwhelming in the best possible way. He whispered things that made her blush as he stripped off her clothes before undressing himself. Then he followed through on a lot of those whispers until Katelyn cried out his name again and again.

His fingers inside of her as his mouth lapped at her clit sent her spiraling over the top, every muscle in her body clenched as she exploded. Her orgasm claimed her as strongly as John had and when she felt the head of his cock pressing into her, she wrapped her arms around him and pressed her hips into him, all but begging for more.

She wanted more of the connection they'd built. Wanted to be closer to him, to be one with him as their bodies raced toward completion again. His eyes didn't leave hers as he sank into her again and again, drawing rasping breaths from her. His length plunging into her lit every nerve ending, bringing pleasure so pure she found herself praying it would never end, but wanting to feel his release just the same.

And then they were there. John cried out and tensed beneath her hands, just as she felt the rippling ecstasy of another orgasm hit her. They came together, the erotic power of knowing she'd brought him to this racing through her even as her own body sang and tingled and melted in his arms.

Snuggling into him afterward, their legs linked under the sheets, Katelyn couldn't remember a time when she'd felt more content, and she knew coming home to Evers had been the right choice after all.

CHAPTER NINETEEN

Charlie Hanford looked up as his housekeeper entered his office. She always seemed to come just when he was getting settled into his work. But he had to hand it to her, she had a rigid routine. She'd kept this place running like clockwork for almost thirty years. She performed all of his routine weekly cleaning on Fridays, but on Mondays, she had her "list" that was not to be disrupted regardless of weather, his schedule, or any other outside force he'd ever been able to find.

On the first Monday of every month, she moved the refrigerator and cleaned behind it and dusted all the blinds in the house. On the second Monday, she vacuumed all of the upholstery and dusted the air vents and ceiling fans. The third Monday was reserved for cleaning the windows and sills. This must be the fourth Monday of the month because she appeared in his office, sandpaper in hand. Time to sand the inside of his cedar chest.

He'd tried to tell her she needn't worry about the cedar chest. But she was adamant. She'd tell him that was where she kept extra blankets and the spare linens for the holiday party, and did he want those all moth eaten every year when they took them out to use them? According to Mrs. Bloom, the way to preserve your cedar chest was to sand the inside a bit each month to maintain the cedar smell.

His look must have told her what he was thinking again. She actually tsked-tsked him, something she did quite frequently. "When you go to sell this place someday, you'll thank me for maintaining it," she said as she lifted the lid. The chest was built into the bay window of his office and really was a nice feature to the room. Maybe she was right. Charlie didn't say anything as she leaned in and began to sand the inside of the cedar planks.

"It was a nice funeral they had for old Alan," she continued her chatter and Charlie nodded. It had been nice.

Mrs. Bloom stood and looked at him. "Had to be hard for you, I suppose. Burying Sam and then Alan so quickly, one right after the other like that."

Charlie frowned and nodded again. What do you say to something like that? It was true. He'd just buried the two men he'd been closest to all these years.

Mrs. Bloom bent to her task again, jabbering as she worked. Charlie almost tuned out as she started talking about poor Katelyn having to bury her father, but the next thing she said stopped his heart cold.

"I remember the way little Katelyn Bowden used to play in here when she was young. She'd tag along with her mama and climb in here to play hide and seek. I'd find her asleep in here sometimes while her mama worked. Good thing she wasn't in here the day poor Caroline was murdered."

Charlie shuffled papers on his desk as the implications of what she'd just said sank in. Alan had never told anyone why he'd sent Katelyn away. Even when Charlie had asked him, he hadn't told him anything more than she belonged with her aunt in Austin. Mrs. Bloom continued to chatter to herself as his mind raced over the details of the day long ago when Caroline had died.

There wasn't a detail of the day Charlie didn't remember, but suddenly one detail meant more than it ever had. Alan had asked to be alone with his wife before the coroner took her away. No one, including Charlie, had thought anything of it. Of course a man would want a minute to say goodbye to his wife.

Charlie had volunteered to stay with him, but Alan had insisted on being alone. Alan had stayed in the office with Caroline's body alone for a long time before leaving with his sister. That might not mean much, but Charlie recalled one fact that hadn't seemed odd at the time. Alan's sister had picked him up at the back door—the door that led out of Charlie's office and straight into the backyard. She'd pulled the car right up to the back and picked him up. Charlie, and everyone else at the time, assumed Alan hadn't wanted to see anyone. Hadn't wanted to face the large group of neighbors and friends gathered at the scene as he crumpled under the weight of his wife's murder. Hadn't wanted them to see him fall.

Now Charlie stared at the papers on his desk, not seeing anything as the blood rushed to his head, making him dizzy with the realization that big, tough Sheriff Alan Bowden probably hadn't been hiding his anguish that day. He'd likely been hiding a secret he hadn't even wanted his best friend to know. Charlie would be willing to bet that little Katelyn Bowden was most likely in the room when Caroline had been killed. Most likely in the chest that Mrs. Bloom stood over right now.

THE HOUSE WAS QUIET. Even though her father had been in the hospital the entire time Katelyn had been back in Evers, somehow, after he died, the house became still and silent in a way it hadn't been before. As if somehow, just knowing her father wouldn't ever come back, had conveyed finality to the emptiness. Katelyn looked around at the living room with her father's worn easy chair and the coffee table that had seen better days a very long time ago. She couldn't decide what to do from here, whether to sell the house and find something newer for herself or whether to settle in and stay. And if she stayed, should she soak up the feel of being surrounded by her father's things, or re-do the house to her tastes.

She walked into the small office her father had off the living room. It was cluttered with stacks of old newspapers and magazines he'd felt the need to keep for one reason or another. There was a shelf behind his desk that held the only pictures of her mother left in the house other than the one on her nightstand. For some reason, her father never seemed to want pictures of her mother around. Katelyn didn't know if it had been too hard for him to see the reminders of the woman he'd loved, or if he'd thought it would be hard on Katelyn on the few occasions she came to visit. The picture of her father and mother on their wedding day and a picture of them holding Katelyn on the day she was born were the only ones he displayed.

John planned to come back and pick her up for dinner at the end of his shift. Katelyn looked at the face of her phone. Two more hours, at least, assuming his shift went smoothly. That was a big "if" for the sheriff of such a large county. So, at a minimum, two hours to kill before dinner with John. Katelyn sighed and pulled open one of the drawers of her father's desk. His lawyer had already come by the day before. The will was clean and easy. Everything was left to her. The house, his small bit of savings, his old truck. Things would be tied up a bit in probate proceedings, but the lawyer expected that all to go seamlessly. There wasn't anyone to contest anything.

Katelyn's phone rang, pulling her from her thoughts.

"Hi, Charlie," Katelyn said after looking at her screen and reading the contact saved as Charlie Hanford. She had saved his information in her phone when her father's dementia got really bad. Charlie had been great about coming by when Katelyn called to say her father was having a rough day. He'd been able to calm her father in a way others hadn't and she was grateful for the friendship he'd given them both in her father's last month.

"How are you doing, Kate? You holding up okay, sweetheart?"

Katelyn smiled sadly. She supposed Charlie was all she had now as far as family, although even as she had the thought, a flash of John's face caused her to warm inside. No, she had a lot more than just Uncle Charlie left. She had new friends, and she had John. She had a home here in Evers.

"I'm doing pretty well. Better than I thought I would, anyway," Katelyn said, with a genuine smile. She was sad for her father and missed him, but his pain and confusion had been so clear at the end. She'd been relieved for him when it ended. Her sorrow was really for herself when she thought about it. For what she'd lost. But wasn't that always the way death was? Harder on those left behind?

"Good, that's good, Kate. You know I'm here if you need anything, right?" he asked.

"Yes, Charlie, thank you. I'll let you know." Katelyn looked around the room and wondered if Charlie might know where to start on her father's belongings. What do you do with the things a person treasured during their life after they died? Should she donate them or select gifts for the people he cared about most?

Surely, there was something here Charlie might want of her father's as a memento? Something that held some memory for them?

Katelyn opened her mouth to ask, but Charlie cut in. "Listen, Katy, I'm looking at the plans Sam drew up here for your studio." Katelyn cringed at his use of the name Katy, but didn't respond. "I'm turning all of his projects over to my new foreman, but I thought I'd take care of your studio myself, personally, that is. For you."

"Oh, um, okay. Thank you. I appreciate that." Katelyn knew the work on her studio had stalled with Sam's passing, but she had been too focused on her father to mind.

"Can you come by my house to take a look at the plans with me? I have some questions for you before we move forward. Things Sam noted, but didn't really explain well. He had his own shorthand that only he understood. Between that and his chicken-scratch handwriting, I can't understand some of the notations he made."

"When did you want me to come by?" Katelyn asked. She'd seen the way Sam scribbled on the edges of the blue-prints and had wondered herself how he'd be able to read it later when the time came. She couldn't imagine someone else trying to decipher it. Hopefully, she'd remember every-thing they talked about when she saw what Charlie was struggling with.

"Could you come by today? I understand if you can't," Charlie started, but Katelyn cut in.

"Now is fine. I can come now," she said, pushing herself

up from her father's desk with no small sense of relief. She'd prefer to throw herself into the building of the studio and get back to her art instead of trying to delve into the decisions she seemed unable to make at home. A distraction right now was exactly what she needed.

"Wonderful," came Charlie's answer as she grabbed her keys and purse and headed for the front door. "I'll see you in a few minutes."

Katelyn knew where he lived. Even someone who hardly spent any time in Evers knew Charlie Hanford owned the big house at the top of Evers Hill. She texted John as she pulled up the long drive leading to the house with its white front porch and limestone exterior.

Ran over to Charlie's to work on studio blueprints. Text when you're ready for dinner?

She didn't wait for a reply. She knew he was often too busy when he was working to respond right away, and she knew his answer would be yes. Slipping her phone in her purse, Katelyn shut the car door and walked up to Charlie's front door. Snippets of the false memory that had plagued Katelyn for years bounced around in her head, but she pushed them aside. There weren't any pine trees around, just as she'd known there wouldn't be.

For years, she'd tried to grasp at the memory. To pull at the strands in her mind to knit a picture together, but there just weren't enough strands. In fact, she wasn't sure she could truly *see* anything. It was more a feeling, or a sense. A *sense* of being in a pine forest, rather than the actual sight of trees.

Katelyn took a deep breath and pushed forward despite the shiver running down her spine, causing an involuntary shudder. Twenty-four years. Surely her mother's ghost was no longer haunting the halls of the house she was about to enter.

"Come in, Katy." Charlie stood on the porch, holding the front door open. She hadn't even realized he was there, and she wondered briefly if he'd seen her fortifying herself.

"Thanks," she murmured as she entered the foyer, feeling the weight of being in his home on her shoulders. She followed Charlie through the entranceway and into a large living room. When he headed toward the French doors, Katelyn knew they would lead to his office, as if instinct or some long-buried memory spoke to her.

She stopped short. She couldn't go in there. Surely, he wouldn't walk her straight into the room where her mother had died. Katelyn's palms grew clammy, and her stomach flipped over, churning with unwelcome nerves she honestly hadn't expected. It had been so long ago. Another lifetime, really.

"Honey, are you okay?" Charlie asked, turning back to peer at her before smacking his forehead in an almost comic-like gesture of stupidity. "What am I thinking? I can't bring you in my office. I'm so sorry," he said, leading her to the couch in the living room.

Katelyn was astonished at how limp she'd become, how pliable she was as Charlie practically pushed her down onto the couch, talking all the time about how thoughtless it had been of him to try to walk her into his office.

"Such habits, Katelyn, I tell you. You get to be my age and you just don't think about things like that anymore. Everything's such a habit. You sit right here. I'll just get the blueprints and bring them out here." He patted her hand and rushed into the office.

As far as Katelyn knew, her father, as close as he was to Charlie, hadn't stepped foot in this house other than during the investigation in the weeks following the murder. He had never come here in all these years. He visited her over the holidays in Austin and always timed his visits with Charlie's holiday party. Katelyn frowned. In fact, it seemed odd now that Charlie would have stayed in the house after what had happened. She'd never given that any thought, but she wondered why he would have stayed after his best friend's wife was murdered in a room he worked in on a daily basis. *Who does that?*

Charlie came in with a roll of papers under one arm and a blanket over the other. He dumped the papers on the coffee table in front of Katelyn then draped the blanket around her shoulders.

"You're still looking pale. I'll get you a glass of water," he said and didn't wait for a response before leaving her again.

Katelyn pulled the blanket tighter around her shoulders, frustrated with her response to simply sitting in Charlie's living room. Just as she was about to tell herself to get it together, the scent hit her. The blanket smelled of pine trees. Katelyn lifted the blanket and took a deep breath. A pine forest. The pine forest of her disconnected memories.

The bottom fell out of Katelyn's stomach as if her whole world had fallen out from under her.

She didn't remember making the conscious decision to go into the office. In fact, if she was thinking at all, she likely would have had the wherewithal to run out the front door. But, her brain wasn't functioning. Some primal memory in the mind of that four-year-old child was at work now. One minute she was on the couch, and the next her hand was on the doorknob to Charlie's office, pushing the door open, knowing she had to see, had to know what she seemed to know in her heart.

She had been here. She *had* seen and heard her mother's murder.

Nothing could have prepared Katelyn for the weak sensation in her knees, the feeling that her world was spinning sideways, as if she were losing her legs beneath her. Her eyes traveled instantly to the chest in the bay window with its brightly colored cushions creating a tempting reading nook. She'd played in it as a child. Of that she was absolutely sure.

Katelyn walked to the chest and lifted the lid, her head whirling dizzily as her mind was assailed with memories and sensations. It was dark. She was in her hiding place when the voices started. She watched through the narrow slits between the boards of the chest. Not through trees in a pine forest. Not pine at all, she realized, now. Cedar. The chest was cedar, designed to preserve the blankets and linens stored in it. Her childish mind must have mistaken the scent for pine and kept that false memory alive all these years.

The memories connected, one to another in her head. The snippets no longer floating, no longer disconnected and unclear. This time, the scenes fell in line in her head as a linear puzzle pieced together. Two faces, two angry voices. Her mother's and Sam Denton's. Her mother's scream as she fell when Sam reached out to grab her. Then a third face, a third voice that sent cold fingers of dread dancing an unwelcome pattern up Katelyn's spine. The shiver she'd felt earlier returned ten-fold.

Charlie. *Uncle* Charlie, asking Sam what happened. Uncle Charlie saying it was too late now. Her mother could not be allowed to wake up. Uncle Charlie hitting her mother repeatedly in the head with a bookend, until no life remained in the still form Katelyn could almost see lying there still on the floor.

For a moment, Katelyn was as frozen in fear as the child-Katelyn had been so many years ago. Frozen and mute and helpless as she recalled Charlie's rushed instructions to ditch the murder weapon. He'd stuffed cash from a box in Sam's hands as he shoved Sam out the door leading to the manicured back lawn of his oversized home.

The memories released their ghostly hold. Katelyn backpedaled. She had to get out of the house now. That much she knew. The voice behind her, the arms grabbing her, much stronger than she'd expect them to be if she stopped to think about it. Strong arms that stopped her heart and stole the breath from her lungs. Uncle Charlie's voice was gone. In its place was nothing but the voice of a psychopath. Like nothing she'd ever heard before. Flat and dead as he spoke so matter-of-factly in her ear, it drew a sort-of panicked giggle from her throat that ended in a choked sob.

"I had to be sure. I couldn't chance it coming out after all these years," he said, with no feeling whatsoever. Simply mild interest. "And, what better way than to see if coming back here triggered any memories for you."

Katelyn lashed out, swinging arms and elbows behind her, trying to break his hold on her, but his grip was strong.

"Now then," he said, with a senseless level of calm that belied the situation. The soothing tone he adopted was nothing short of sick. Katelyn felt her stomach clench.

"We can't very well do this here. Although there is a hint of romance to it, people would probably catch on if you were found dead in the very spot where your mother was murdered. Even I would have a hard time making that look like an accident, and I have to say, I'm beginning to excel at getting away with murder. It's beautiful, really, if you think about it."

"It's disgusting is what it is," Katelyn spat. Her stomach protested the thought that she might not get away from him, sending a wave of bile up her throat. "Sick and disgusting, just like you."

She threw her head back hoping to connect with his head. If she did, she'd probably only succeed in knocking herself out, but she tried anyway. She had to try everything she could to get out of this. She remembered something about the importance of not letting an abductor remove you from the initial scene. Something about the chances of death increasing exponentially after you were moved.

Hopeless as it was, she threw her head back, but only met his shoulder. He laughed, the cruelty in his tone almost stunning, given what she'd come to associate with Charlie Hanford. The whole town saw him as the supportive, benevolent benefactor he'd always portrayed himself to be. There was none of that in him now as he dragged her through his office and out onto the back lawn. Katelyn kicked out, knocking over a flower pot that sat next to the door. Her only chance if she couldn't stop him was to leave a sign for John, some clue that she'd been taken, and pray he could find her.

As Charlie dragged her to his car, Katelyn fought his hold, digging her heels into the soft dirt to leave furrows of evidence. She kicked out at the planter that stood at the end of the path, but missed. The driveway was paved. She was running out of opportunities to leave signals for John. She kicked off a shoe as Charlie opened the trunk of his car and shoved her in. Panic flooded her. She didn't start breathing again until the trunk slammed and she realized she was shut in its coffin-like interior. There could be no more signaling John. If he was going to figure out she was in trouble, he'd have to do it with the clues she'd left already. She had to hope he'd come to Charlie's place and then find some way to track her once he figured out Charlie had taken her.

The whole thing was hopeless. How could John track where Charlie took her? Katelyn choked on a sob, but focused on her breathing and tried to calm herself. The darkness of the trunk overwhelmed her. She was filled with dread, realizing Charlie could take her anywhere he wanted and she'd be defenseless when he opened the trunk. Katelyn felt around her, trying to find something, anything, to use as a weapon, but the trunk was empty. Of course it was. He'd planned this.

Her mind raced back to an old TV show. One of those Worst Case Scenario episodes. It had showed what to do if you're locked in a trunk. *Yes!* There should be a safety release latch in all new cars. Katelyn felt for a latch on the side of the trunk. Nothing.

She shifted and twisted, wincing as the car hit a bump, tossing her up to the ceiling of the cramped space. She kept moving, doubted she had much time. Katelyn's hands found the flap that should have covered the safety release, but there was no release. Had he removed it?

Not a problem, she told herself, attempting to force her stomach to stop the roiling flips it was doing. She took a breath to steady her hands as she thought back to the TV show she'd only barely watched.

Not a problem? What am I, nuts?

The girl trapped in the trunk had done some trick where she pulled the wires of the taillight out and made it blink to get people's attention, or to try to get a passing police officer to pull the car over. Katelyn couldn't for the life of her remember how the girl had done it, but she would try. The car slowed and then turned. The turn and the bumps in the road combined to toss her sideways. They had to be on a dirt road.

She scrambled back, trying to balance herself, focusing on getting into the guts of the taillights. She didn't make it far. The car stopped, and Katelyn braced herself for a face-off with Charlie. She might have nothing to fight with other than her fists or nails or feet, but she'd fight.

As the trunk opened, Katelyn was blinded by the sudden light. She swung her arms and scratched at Charlie's face as he yanked her out. He dropped her to the ground and kicked her in the side. Katelyn curled in a ball against the blow and tried to get her bearings. Nothing but dry, dusty dirt and quiet all around them. Of course, he had brought her somewhere isolated.

Charlie hauled Katelyn up by the arms and she saw where they were. A construction site. One apparently abandoned. He grasped her arm, shoving her toward one of the half-completed buildings. He was a lot stronger than she would have guessed for his age. Her mind seemed to be focusing on all the wrong things even though everything within her was screaming she'd be dead in minutes if she didn't do something.

"You should have stayed in Austin," Charlie said, as he wrenched her arm viciously. She tried not to cry out, but the pain engulfed her. Her scream seemed to egg him on. "A few more years and I would have been out of here. I would have retired before anyone knew what had happened. But you just couldn't stay away, could you?"

Katelyn thought about telling him she wouldn't say

anything, that she would never tell his secrets, but he wasn't stupid. He wouldn't believe her after things had come this far.

She pretended to trip and fell to the ground, praying she could make this work. When Charlie reached down to grab her again, she jabbed her thumbs into his eyes as hard as she could. Nails out, thumbs braced to inflict maximum damage. She raked her fingers down his face, digging in with her nails. It wasn't pleasant, but if the pained howl he let loose was an indication, she'd been effective. Katelyn shoved back, pushing herself out from under him.

She kicked out with one leg, knocked him down, then turned and ran, stumbling for a second before gaining her footing. She ran for the road, unsure how she'd get away. They were so far away from anything and anyone. And she was on foot, while he had the car and could hunt her down. She ran blindly, resisting the urge to look back to see if he was coming. She was a runner. Surely she was in better shape than he was, even if he was a lot stronger.

Katelyn focused on moving, intent on getting out of this alive. She would not die at the hands of her mother's killer, the man who had already taken so much from her.

JOHN SMILED as he read the text from Katelyn. Dinner sounded like just what he needed right now and he couldn't wait to get back to her. The phone rang before he put it back down.

"This is John Davies," he said.

"John, it's Catherine Tanner. I got back some of the results from the scenes we've processed. What do you want first? Info from Sam Denton's scene or info on Ken Statler?"

"Start with Sam. Anything usable there?" John asked.

"No prints anywhere you wouldn't expect them, from people you wouldn't expect to be there. Prints on the blockade that should have been up around the elevator shaft, but they belong to the construction guys and Charlie Hanford, so nothing unusual there and no evidence of tampering. Either he threw himself at those wooden barricades or someone else did it for him. I guess if he was really drunk, he could have fallen against them hard enough to break through them, but I ran his blood. Nothing. No alcohol, no drugs. Nothing."

"Hmm. Danny spoke with friends, neighbors, people he worked with and no one reported the kind of thing Charlie said he witnessed. Is it possible for you to check for dementia now?" John asked, wondering if he should really be spending county resources this way. Something about the way this case wrapped itself up in a nice neat bow with Sam Denton's death didn't sit well with him. He couldn't say for sure what it was, but there was still some small whisper of doubt. He'd feel a lot better if they had clear evidence of either a suicide or an accident.

"Sure, I can look at the brain again, study it closer for any signs of degeneration," Catherine said.

"Okay. Do that. What did you find at the Statler scene? Anything useful?"

"Nothing we didn't already know. I pulled the bookend from the scene of Caroline Bowden's murder out of storage. They do appear to be a matching set. I sent the one we pulled out of the pond to Austin. Just as we thought—no useable DNA, prints, fibers. Nothing. Same with the chain that Ken's body was wrapped in. Whoever lashed him to that steering wheel either wore gloves, or any DNA and prints were washed away over the years."

"Okay. Anything else?" John asked, anxious to get back to Katelyn to see how she was doing. He hated leaving her so soon after her father's death.

"Cause of death was likely drowning. The blow to the head wouldn't have killed him."

"Okay, thanks, Cathy." John hung up and sat staring out the windshield of his cruiser for a minute. Something wasn't right, that much he knew. He just needed to figure out what was actually giving him this gut feeling.

He muttered a curse under his breath and started the car. Time to put the case out of his mind for the evening. He turned out onto the highway and headed over to meet Katelyn at Charlie's place.

He'd see if she felt up to going out to dinner. Maybe they'd even drive over to Johnson City and eat somewhere nicer than Two Sisters Diner or Tiny Bob's.

It didn't take long for him to realize dinner wouldn't be happening. There was no answer at Charlie's even though Katelyn's car sat out front. When John went around back, his blood ran cold. The door to Charlie's office stood open. One of the flower pots was overturned and there were clear marks of someone being dragged from the house. And suddenly, the pieces John hadn't been able to see clicked into place. He'd thought everything around Caroline Bowden's death was connected to Sam Denton, but everything was equally connected to Charlie Hanford. He'd been stupid not to see it before. Sam Denton and Ken Statler had both worked for Charlie, just as Caroline had. She'd been found in Charlie's office.

John let fly a string of curses, directed mostly at himself for not seeing what now seemed so obvious. But if Alan hadn't seen it, hell, maybe John had just picked up Alan's blinders where Charlie was concerned. They'd both obviously missed one hell of a big signal.

He radioed for Danny and Carter Jenkins to head toward Charlie's house, then jumped on the radio to Berta.

"Berta, does your sister's husband still work for Charlie Hanford?" he asked without worrying about greetings.

"Sure does."

"Get him on the phone and find out where Charlie's got projects. I need to know every site he has active, everything they're working on." A thought occurred. "And, first priority, find out if there's anything they're not working on. Any projects on hold or delayed? Anything that wouldn't have anyone on site today."

"You got it, boss," Berta said and John slowly walked the scene again, taking in every detail as he waited to hear back. He didn't know what had happened, but his gut told him Charlie had Kate and he had to get to her before it was too late. If there'd been any doubt in John's mind that he loved

Katelyn, that he wanted to spend his life with her, it was gone now.

His heart clenched as he made himself ignore the possibility that he might not get to her in time. He didn't have a choice. There'd be no coming back from this one. If she died, he died, too.

CHAPTER TWENTY

John watched Danny pull up the drive at Charlie's house just as he was walking back out to the front. "How long ago did he grab her?" Danny asked.

"She texted me an hour ago when she arrived here. They could be anywhere by now," John said. The men were grim and silent. They both knew what could happen in an hour.

Carter pulled din just as Berta radioed back with her sister's husband, Gordo, on the line. Without preamble, Gordo listed properties Charlie Hanford's company was working on.

"Gordo," John cut in, "which ones aren't currently active or not being worked, today?"

"Two of them. We're waiting on some zoning approvals at a home site off Palmer Drive near the elementary school."

John shook his head even though Gordo couldn't see him. "Too close to town. Where's the other one?"

"A small set of rental houses out on Edge Road. The owner lost his funding so the project is on hold until everything is sorted out, or Charlie decides to buy out the owner and complete the project on his own. It's pretty damned isolated. There's nothing else out that way."

John was halfway to his SUV before Gordo finished, with Danny and Carter following.

"Carter, head to the Palmer Drive site in case I'm wrong," John called over his shoulder. "Danny, you follow me to Edge Road."

"You got it, boss," the men called in overlapping answer.

John ate up the road, heading for the highway out to the long dirt road that would lead them to the site. There were a lot of remote locations in the Hill Country and this was certainly one of them. John just prayed he would reach Katelyn in time.

He gritted his teeth as the car fishtailed when he took a turn too fast. Not reaching her in time wasn't an option. It simply *wasn't* an option.

KATELYN FELT the burn in her lungs as she pushed her body to keep going, running hard across grass flattened by construction machinery and the boots of men who'd been here days ago. There wasn't anyone here now. No one in sight.

Her feet hit the dirt road. She powered through the pain as rocks cut into her bare feet. Focused all her energy on moving forward, churning her legs, trying to eat up ground faster than she realistically could. The distance to any populated place was too great, but she pushed on anyway. Fighting him had proven hopeless. She had to keep moving.

She heard the sound of a car coming up behind her. Fast. Charlie! Katelyn veered off the road and headed into a field, running hard toward a stand of trees. Her mind raced. There'd been no fence, so she wouldn't likely to run into any cattle. She had no idea what a bull might do if she entered its field, but she'd worry about that later.

If she could make it to the trees, Charlie would have to get out and chase her on foot, making the fight a little more even. She focused on nothing but the trees. Coming closer, at an impossibly slow rate. Her breath grew ragged. She forced herself to steady it, churning her legs as fast as she could.

She chanced a glance over her shoulder, saw his car plowing through the field after her. He'd had to slow on the rough ground considering his sedan wasn't suited to off-roading. Katelyn ran through the trees, feeling branches lash at her arms. The stand of trees thinned, and she had to cross a large patch of open land again. She glanced back and saw Charlie doing just what she'd thought he would; circling wide and cutting to the open area, nearly catching up to her as she broke through and raced for the next patch of trees. She heard a loud clank and looked back. The car had bottomed out in one of the large pitted areas that were hard to see. Thankfully, it didn't look like he could keep going. She didn't know if it was a blown tire or the rut itself that trapped the car, but Charlie was now on foot.

Katelyn angled back toward the road. Now that Charlie was running, she wanted to get back to relatively flat ground and try to flag down help. Although she hadn't been jogging much lately, with her father's illness, back in Austin she'd run five to seven miles at a time. She tried to estimate how far she was from town. Charlie had driven at least twenty minutes. That was a lot more miles than she could run, but maybe she could get to a busier road where someone would see her.

Ten yards from the road, Katelyn knew she wasn't going to make it. It wasn't that she gave up. She would never stop fighting.

It was the rock or branch that her foot hit. The sound, like popping ice cubes, meant her ankle was done.

She cried out in pain and anger as she went down. Cried out in pain, and anger, and utter frustration. Flipping onto her butt, she pulled her leg in close and looked around. She barely had a moment to register how close Charlie was before he was on top of her.

His face was red with rage and his eyes swollen almost closed. He gave a guttural scream as he flung himself on her and went for her neck. Katelyn tried to kick him with her good leg, but his hands found their mark. The crush of his hands on her neck, the shocking pain as his grip closed, sent Katelyn into panic. This couldn't happen. She wouldn't let it.

She tried to pry his hands away, but her efforts were

futile. She flung her arms out and wildly felt for anything she could use as a weapon. Her hands touched the cold hard surface of a rock. She grasped it with waning strength and hit Charlie in the side of the head as hard as she could.

Unfortunately, her best wasn't very hard at this point. She was losing strength and consciousness more quickly than she thought she would.

The blow stunned Charlie for a moment. He eased up on her throat briefly. Katelyn sucked in a small amount of air, tried to twist out of his hold, but he tightened his grip once more. She hit him again and again. If he killed her, she'd make damn sure she went down fighting; make damn sure there'd be evidence of a fight that he'd have to explain away. He wouldn't walk away free after killing her. Wouldn't go on living without punishment, like he'd done to her mother.

John spotted the tangled bodies of Katelyn and her attacker on the side of the road. He was too far away to see if she was alive, if she still had a chance. They were still a couple of miles out from the construction site, so she must have run. Must have been trying to get away. He'd known Katelyn would fight back. John jumped from the truck as he said a silent prayer her fight had been enough, that he'd made it to her in time.

He gripped Charlie by the shoulders and threw him off her, launching him as hard and as far as he could. Danny

213

would deal with him, cuff him and get him in the cruiser before John hurt him. John reached for Katelyn.

She lay still on the ground, angry red welts and ugly bruises already forming on her neck. Berta had already dispatched an ambulance to follow them to the site, but John radioed for its arrival time as he dropped to his knees in front of Katelyn.

"Katelyn. Katelyn! Talk to me, baby."

She didn't wake up. John bent his head and listened. Shallow breaths. His fingers found her pulse.

Alive. The rush of relief almost crushed him.

He raised her chin and made sure her airway was as open as it could be as he listened for the sound of sirens. John would have liked to think he kept his head and stayed calm but the truth was, when the EMTs arrived, they had to drag him away from her so they could work to open her airway and get her on a backboard. He knew better. He knew her spine had to be stabilized. He knew she needed oxygen and that her larynx might be crushed, blocking her windpipe. But letting her go almost killed him.

When Danny finally helped them pull him away, he realized he'd been yelling her name the whole time, calling to her to wake her up and bring her back to him. The thought of living without Katelyn by his side, of waking up without her in his life tomorrow. That just wasn't something he could even let himself think about.

CHAPTER TWENTY-ONE

John watched Katelyn's breathing. He'd been staring at the machines that monitored her vital signs and the rise and fall of her chest for hours as she slept. The cop in him wanted to be the one to question Charlie Hanford, to wrap up the case and tie up all the loose ends and unanswered questions, but he couldn't leave Katelyn. He couldn't let her wake up alone.

The door opened quietly and Danny poked his head in, a question in his eyes.

John nodded and stepped to the door, speaking in a hushed voice. "Anything yet?"

"Charlie's not talking. Just asked for his lawyer, then shut up. I went over to talk to Mrs. J. I thought maybe we might get something from her since everyone's always thought Katelyn was with her when Caroline Bowden was murdered," Danny whispered, and both men looked over their shoulders at the woman sleeping in the bed.

"She have anything new to say?" John asked.

Danny nodded. "A lot. Turns out, she's been covering for Alan all these years. He asked her to lie and say Katelyn was with her so no one would ever guess she'd witnessed the murder. She said Alan told her he questioned Katelyn, but she was too traumatized to tell him anything. He didn't see the point in letting anyone know she was a witness since she couldn't tell them anything anyway. Said it would only harm her and possibly put her in danger."

"It's a good thing, since his best friend was the killer, with access to Katelyn," John said, although a big part of him wished Alan had told him this years before. Maybe they could have solved this case with Katelyn's help before her life had been put in danger.

"Mrs. J. agreed to keep it a secret and she's kept it all these years. When I told her about Charlie and how he'd gone after Katelyn, she didn't see that it would help to keep the secret anymore."

Both men were quiet for a minute before Danny whispered, "How's she doing?" with a nod to the bed.

"She'll be fine, the doctors said. She won't be able to eat solid food for a while, and her voice may be permanently dam...changed from the attack." He'd been about to say damaged like the doctors had, but he didn't see it as damaged. Katelyn was here and alive. She might sound different, but he wouldn't care about that, and he didn't want her feeling like there was anything wrong with sounding different. "She'll be able to check out in a few days," he finished, and then he heard a strangled sob from the bed and realized Katelyn had woken up.

Danny slipped out the door, letting it swing shut behind him as John went to the bed where Katelyn lay quietly crying. He slipped his hand in hers, threading their fingers together and squeezing gently.

"Don't try to talk for now, baby. It's going to be a few days before they even want you to try talking." Katelyn's eyes looked wild and panicked for a minute, but John leaned in and kissed her lips softly, whispering against them, "It's all right. I'm here. I'm not going anywhere."

John held her while she cried for a long time. He knew she was crying because her father's best friend had betrayed him. Because her mother had died at the hands of a man so close to their family. Because she was scared and didn't want to feel the way she was feeling. He knew she was crying because of the way it felt to imagine never seeing John again, just the way it had torn at his heart when he'd had to imagine never seeing her again. She cried for her mother and for the time she'd lost with her father. She cried for all those things and more.

And John held her.

CHAPTER TWENTY-TWO

Katelyn woke in John's arms and snuggled deeper. She knew the town was talking about the way he'd all but moved into her house, but she didn't care. And, he refused to leave, telling everyone she needed someone there to take care of her while she recovered. He was the only thing holding her together when she woke up from a nightmare in a cold sweat, or worse, when she didn't wake up on her own. He woke her and calmed her down and held her while she fell back to sleep. If she didn't have John there with her, she knew the trauma would be worse.

She'd spent almost a week in the hospital with John sleeping in the chair next to her. The doctors watched her to be sure her breathing wouldn't become compromised as a result of the damage to her larynx, or that she wouldn't develop aspiration pneumonia or any number of other complications they'd rattled off to her. During the hospital stay, Katelyn had tried to avoid looking in the mirror. Her neck was marred with bruises, but also with the claw marks where she'd tried to pull Charlie's hands off and ended up cutting herself. Looking at those marks reminded her too much of the feeling of struggling to take a breath and believing she wouldn't make it away alive.

Katelyn had been stunned to have visits from Ashley every day, and from Laura and Cora several times during the week. Ashley lectured her about her laziness. She told her every day it was time to get up out of bed, but she said it with a grin that told Katelyn she didn't really mean it. The visits made her laugh, which was painful, but they also kept her from sitting and staring at the wall wondering over and over again how everyone in the town could have been so fooled by Charlie Hanford.

The sharp pain in her neck when Ashley made her laugh was a fair trade-off for getting her mind off the man who'd killed her mother and tried to kill her. And, Katelyn had to admit, she'd been really touched when they'd all been so great about visiting. She'd expected one token visit, at best, not repeated visits that seemed to indicate they really cared for her.

"Mornin', baby," John said as he woke and began trailing his hands over her arms, her back. His touch always melted her, turned her to putty in his arms and set her on fire all at once. They hadn't made love since she'd come home from the hospital, though. Her ankle was still in an air cast, and she had to whisper instead of speak, but with John's hands touching her, all thoughts of protecting her ankle or taking precautions with her breathing flew out the window.

Katelyn moaned and shifted to align their bodies, drawing a deep growl from John, but he pulled back.

"Not yet, Katelyn. I don't want to hurt you."

"You'll hurt me more by staying away," she whispered, pulling him back with one hand to his shoulder while the other slid down his chest, reveling in the feel of the muscles that rippled under a threadbare Sheriff's Department T-shirt. The feel of his body and what touching him did to her never ceased to amaze her.

His eyes were dark and dangerous looking as he watched her, clearly trying to resist, but losing the battle as she let her hand drop lower. John rolled them so they lay side by side, then slipped their clothes off slowly, so tenderly Katelyn almost laughed at the idea of big strong Sheriff John Davies being so gentle. Before she could finish the thought, he stole her breath and she melted into him, swept away with the sensation of their bodies melding as he took her to places no other man had ever taken her.

JOHN BRACED his hands on his desk, leaning over it to be sure the lawyer standing across from him understood every word he said.

"She deserves answers. Hell, the whole town deserves answers. They've waited twenty-four years to know who killed one of our own, and it turned out to be a man we all trusted and respected."

Reese Cutter stared at John, unspeaking for an

awkwardly long pause, but John held the assistant district attorney's gaze. He wasn't going to back down until Katelyn had answers about her mother's death.

Cutter relented. "I'll give it a shot, but I have to prioritize getting information about Sol City out of him. Whatever they did to cut corners on the project could put peoples' lives in danger. Sam Denton's dead; the building inspector we suspect must have been in on it is dead. The only one with any answers is Charlie Hanford. I have to put the safety of the residents at Sol City ahead of getting answers for Katelyn. But..." Cutter raised his hand in response to John's obvious rising anger and said more emphatically, "But I'll do all I can to get answers for Katelyn. That's all I can promise."

John's jaw clenched as he followed Cutter down the hall to the room where Charlie Hanford and his lawyer waited. He stepped into the observation room as Cutter continued on to the doorway leading to interrogation. John would listen in, but wouldn't be in the room. It killed him to leave Hanford up to Cutter instead of being in there himself. But if he did anything stupid—like go after Charlie Hanford the way he wanted to—Caroline's killer could walk and Katelyn would never get justice.

He watched as Cutter tossed down photocopies of the double set of books they'd found hidden in Charlie's house. Then he listened as Cutter laid out the case against Hanford for Caroline Bowden's murder, the fraud charges related to the building of Sol City, Sam Denton's murder, and the kidnapping and attempted murder of Katelyn

Bowden. That part still sent a cold rush through John's blood.

Cutter threw in charges for Ken Statler's murder. They could charge Charlie with Ken's murder even if, as they suspected, Sam Denton had been the one to kill him. Because the murder had happened as part of a plot to commit felony fraud, Charlie Hanford could be held liable for that murder, just as if he had been the one to hit Ken in the head and drown him. Then Cutter made their one and only pitch for getting the answers they needed. He took the death penalty off the table. Facing three counts of murder in Texas meant the death penalty was very much in play, and very much a realistic outcome of the case.

John held his breath, arms crossed tensely across his chest, as he ground his teeth together. Hanford's defense attorney whispered in Hanford's ear, but it didn't take long for him to cave. As John watched, Hanford laid out the details of Caroline's and Ken's murders, that of the housing inspector years before, then Sam's, before walking Cutter through the blueprints of Sol City, showing him step-by-step where they'd cut corners.

Hanford tried to tell Cutter that nothing they did would cause any harm to anyone, but John doubted that was true. More than likely, he'd planned to retire and move away before the repercussions started. If Katelyn hadn't come back to town, Charlie would probably have retired in the next few years, disappearing before anyone figured out there were problems at Sol City.

There would be a lot of elderly people displaced while

repairs were made. In fact, John bet it was a miracle none of the structures had collapsed already. Hanford and Denton had cut a lot of corners and broken a lot of rules on that job. And that was likely just the beginning. Hanford and his company had built a lot of buildings in this area. Everything would need to be inspected. Some might end up condemned.

As John walked out to his car, he couldn't even begin to fathom the necessary cleanup. They not only needed to deal with making sure the cut corners didn't hurt anyone, they had to figure out which of the other construction workers and crew were in on the scheme. No way Charlie and Sam could have gotten away with this without a lot of people turning a blind eye, or taking orders without bothering to question what was being done. According to Charlie, that was what had gotten Ken Statler killed. He had questioned them. He'd challenged Sam and Charlie, and they had taken him out the same day they killed Katelyn's mother. A whole lot of death and lives ruined for what, in the end, amounted to relatively little money. They'd skimmed about five hundred thousand dollars off that job. Five hundred thousand for two lives.

KATELYN WAITED OUTSIDE for John to swing by the house after his shift so they could head over to the potluck dinner Laura and May Bishop had thrown together. He'd worked all day the day before, followed by a morning shift today so they hadn't seen each other for more than a quick good morning before he went to work. Katelyn blushed at the memory. It really hadn't been *that* quick, and it had certainly started her day off right.

She balanced the green salad she'd made on her hip and checked her phone when it beeped indicating a text coming in.

On your way, Kit Kat?

Katelyn smiled and texted Ashley back with one hand. *Waiting for John to pick me up. C u soon:)*

A minute later the phone beeped again.

K! C u:)

Everyone had made a real point to include Katelyn after her ordeal. She had a feeling they wanted to be sure she didn't think about running back to Austin now that her father was gone and the mystery of her mother's death was solved. But, Katelyn was in no danger of heading back to Austin. She'd found a lot more here in Evers than she'd ever thought possible. She had close friends, a man she loved... Yes, she'd decided to admit it to herself even though she had yet to tell John exactly how she felt—and she would have a studio soon.

She was smiling when John pulled his cruiser to the curb in front of her house. He came around to open the door for her and dropped a kiss to her lips. "You look happy. What's got you smiling?" he asked.

"Everything," Katelyn said as she slid into the passenger seat and balanced the salad on her lap.

John seemed to hesitate as he slipped behind the wheel,

and Katelyn felt a rock settle in her stomach when he didn't immediately pull out onto the street.

"What's wrong?" she asked quietly, as he clenched and unclenched the wheel.

John cut the ignition and turned to face her. "I just... I have news about the case, but I don't want to ruin your good mood."

She smiled and shook her head. "Nothing's gonna kill my mood. You can tell me."

"The assistant district attorney got Charlie to talk," John said quietly, watching her face to gauge her reaction.

Katelyn felt as if someone had punched her in the stomach. All the air went out of her lungs at once. She felt as if she might throw up. But she sucked in a deep breath and met John's eyes. "Tell me."

"Charlie and Sam had been skimming from jobs for years. Using shoddy materials, cutting the thickness of concrete slabs, that kind of thing. In the late eighties, Charlie won the bid to build Sol City, the big retirement community outside of town." John paused and waited for Katelyn's nod.

She knew the place. It was a large community with houses, apartments, and a nursing home all in one setting. Elderly residents could start out in a house, then move to an apartment when they needed assisted living, then move to the nursing home if they ever needed full-time care. The place was enormous, with its own grocery store, a golf course and tennis courts, fitness center, medical clinic, the works. It had been Charlie's claim to fame.

"Charlie had been bribing a local zoning inspector for years. The three got together and expanded the little bit of fraud they'd gotten away with on other projects and made it a wholesale scam on that one. They paid a cut to the guys who worked for them back then. Paid off the right people to look the other way. It was a time when there was a lot of corruption around here. They were able to get away with things they probably couldn't get away with now."

John squeezed Katelyn's hand and she remembered to keep breathing.

"Ken Statler apparently started asking questions. They'd offered him money, but it was beginning to look like he couldn't be paid off. Then your mom discovered the two sets of books Charlie was keeping. Sam was at Charlie's office making sure the set of books your mom worked on— the one that looked legit to anyone who went over it—had all the info she needed in it to work on the next day. He went to the kitchen to get a drink and left the books out. Your mom showed up a day early and discovered them sitting out."

"She couldn't be bought, either," Katelyn whispered, not bothering to swipe at the tears that ran down her cheeks. She'd wanted answers for so long. But, she never imagined anything like this.

"No." John shook his head. "She couldn't. Sam found her, and she refused to be bought. He said he was going to call Charlie to come talk to her, but she said Sam needed to leave. I imagine at that point, she was desperately trying to figure out how to get you out of there safely."

Katelyn closed her eyes. She'd been in the cedar chest. Her mom wouldn't have been able to walk away. If Katelyn hadn't been with her, would her mom have been able to run, to fight?

John must have read her mind. "He wouldn't have let her leave that room no matter what. It wasn't because of you. Two very greedy men killed your mom. Sam panicked and grabbed for her. She fell and hit the corner of the desk, but she was still alive. He called Charlie and told him to come home. When Charlie got there, your mom was unconscious but alive. He couldn't let her wake up."

"So she was unconscious when he killed her?" Katelyn asked. Her memories of the event were still vague. Knowing that helped somehow. It would have been worse if her mother was awake and aware she was dying. It was a tiny little strand of good in this whole craptacular web that had been Katelyn's life for the last twenty-four years, but she clung to it.

"Yes. Charlie staged it to look like she'd walked in on a burglar, then Sam made sure Ken Statler disappeared on the same day to throw suspicion toward him," John said.

"Was it Charlie who tried to run me off the road? Who attacked me at the studio?" she asked.

"He says that was Sam. That Sam started to panic when you came back to town. Charlie told him to lay low, just wait it out, but Sam was too nervous. He thought they should chase you out of town. That's why Charlie killed Sam. To stop him from letting their secret out after all these years."

Katelyn nodded then met his eyes with one last question. "How much money did they steal? How much money did they kill my mom for?" The last words came out on a choked sob. John pulled her into his arms and held her. He didn't answer, and she was beyond caring. It didn't matter. No amount of money was worth the pain she and her father had lived with. John shushed her and held her while she cried, but Katelyn didn't allow herself to cry for long. She didn't want to give anything more to Charlie and Sam than they'd already taken from her.

She pushed herself up, took a few deep breaths, and wiped the tears staining her cheeks. It was done. She knew why her father had sent her away, why her mother had been killed. As she stared out the windshield at her father's house, the home where she should have grown up, she knew it was finally over. Katelyn felt as though a rock that had been pressing on her chest for years was lifted away. She let out a deep, slow breath and turned to John.

"Okay," she said with a nod, earning a quizzical look.

"Okay?" he asked, eyebrows raised.

Katelyn nodded. "Okay." Another deep breath and she was ready to face the world. Her cell phone beeped.

Did you two get sidetracked:)

Katelyn laughed and showed her phone to John. "Ashley's waiting for us."

John leaned across the seat and brushed his hand down the side of her face, causing that instant lean into him that made him smile. He kissed her slow and long and so tenderly she thought she just might melt, then pulled back and looked into her eyes.

"Okay," he said with a whole lot more meaning in that single word than its small size indicated and pulled away from the curb.

CHAPTER TWENTY-THREE

I t felt really good to be around her friends, laughing and relaxing and, for once in a very long while, not having a care in the world. Katelyn leaned back in her chair at May Bishop's kitchen table and laughed as Laura told them all about Jamie's attempt to catch a frog the night before with Cade. Laura and Cade's dog, Red, lay at Laura's feet, but she raised her head at the laughter, watching them all as though she wondered what she'd missed.

When the laughter ended, May turned to Katelyn. "So, how are you holding up? John said you were having some pain in your throat? Is it still bothering you?"

Katelyn nodded. "Just a little," she said, glad to have her voice almost back to one hundred percent. "It's not steady. It's just shooting pains from time to time. The doctors say it can last a long time, but it will eventually go away. But other than that, I'm almost completely back to normal. Eating solid food," she said with a grin. Solid food was something she'd never take for granted again.

"And your studio is almost ready, right?" Ashley asked.

"Mmm-hmm. The guys who bought it say they'll have it ready in another week for me. I can't wait to get back to work."

Laura turned to May. "The Hart brothers bought a few of Charlie Hanford's commercial properties. They're going into business together."

Charlie Hanford was selling off properties left and right to pay for his criminal defense lawyer.

May smiled, but there was something mysterious to it. "Are they now?" she asked.

Laura smiled at her mother-in-law. "Did you have something to do with that?"

May shrugged. "I suggested they might try their hand at real estate. Those boys needed something to keep them busy, and this seemed like a good way for them to get back on their feet."

Laura leaned in and kissed May on the cheek as she peeled and sliced the last of the apples for a homemade pie. "And I'll just bet you gave them a little seed money for the project while you were at it." May didn't answer. "You're a good woman, May Bishop."

Ashley explained. "The Hart brothers have been sort of...floundering, you might say. And May likes to help out anyone who seems to need a little push or a little guidance."

"Well I, for one, appreciate them. They've been on top of things at the studio. I was so relieved when I heard someone had bought the building and I'd still have my space," Katelyn said.

Cora poked her head into the kitchen from the backyard. "Hey, guys. We miscalculated the number of hamburger buns we'll need. Can one of you text Shane and ask him to bring about a dozen more?" she asked.

"I got it," Katelyn said, picking up John's cell phone. He'd tossed it and his keys on top of her purse when they came in, before joining the rest of the group outside in the yard. Katelyn still hadn't entered everyone's numbers into her phone so it wasn't unusual for her to grab his phone to text one of their friends.

"Thanks," Cora said as she ducked back outside.

Katelyn froze as she pulled up the message screen and selected Shane's name. She didn't mean to see the history, but when it was laid out for her on the screen, it was hard not to miss. And there, plain as day, Shane had texted John yesterday asking if he wanted to grab lunch. John's reply, despite the fact that he'd told her he was working all day, indicated he was down in San Antonio. No denying the text right in front of her:

Can't. In San Antonio for the day. Call you later.

Katelyn swallowed and stilled the slight shake in her hand. She sent a quick text to Shane about the hamburger buns and put the phone down on top of her purse.

"You okay, Kit Kat?" Ashley asked, studying her from across the table.

Katelyn nodded and smiled. "I'm fine, just a bit tired," she said, but on the inside her head was spinning. She flashed right back to the humiliating moment when she'd discovered Devan had lied to her; that he'd had a wife and child the whole time they were together. Her mind raced as she remembered all the red flags she should have heeded but had somehow ignored. All the signs that should have told her he was lying.

And she knew flat out John had lied to her about yesterday. San Antonio was well outside his jurisdiction. If he had to go there for work, wouldn't he have mentioned it? You don't take a four-hour trip and not mention it unless you're hiding something.

The back door opened and John stepped through, his eyes immediately catching Katelyn's and locking them to his. It was the effect he always had on her. And in that moment, she knew. Knew in her heart—he wasn't Devan. Never mind the fact that her father had trusted this man with his position as sheriff. Never mind that Evers, Texas was so small no one could hide a secret for long. She didn't need any of that to tell her she could trust this man.

And she wouldn't let Devan or the more recent betrayal by Charlie ruin that for her.

"You okay, beautiful?" he murmured as he slid into a seat next to her and put one hand on her leg.

She smiled at him and nodded. "I'm wonderful. I heard there's a shortage of hamburger buns causing a riot outside, though. Shouldn't you be out there laying down the law and all that?" she asked, laughing at the scowl she got in response from him.

"I'm off duty, woman," he said, then reached for his

phone. "I came in to text Shane to see if he can get more rolls."

"Already texted him," Katelyn said, and she saw the moment when his eyes saw her text and he processed what she'd seen. He froze. If anyone else in the kitchen had seen it, they didn't let on. John looked up at her and she could see the stricken expression in his eyes. She could read the panic. He had to know she would figure out the lie the minute she saw Shane and his texts.

"Kate..." he started.

She leaned into him, lacing one arm around his neck to pull his ear in close. "I'm fine. Perfect. Wonderful. I promise," she whispered and then pulled back to let him see her eyes, to let him know she was telling the truth. She *really* was okay. Because she trusted him. "Tell me about it later," she said with a small kiss.

The look on his face was almost comical. "Okay," he said, drawing out the word. "We're good?"

"Very good. Go back outside. We'll be out with more food in just a bit," she said, her smile genuine.

EPILOGUE

John didn't tell Katelyn the whole story later that evening. He told her part of it. The part where he planned to take her on a surprise trip to San Antonio the following weekend. He wouldn't tell her why he'd needed to go all the way there to plan their trip ahead of time. He didn't tell her what he had in store for her. But, she was okay with that.

And, the story would make for a great one to tell the grandkids someday. John had planned a weekend on the River Walk in San Antonio—a river lined with hotels, restaurants, and walkways. A river steeped in romance. He had booked a room in one of the oldest hotels along the river, and made a reservation for dinner at one of the fancier restaurants. But it was the detour on the way to dinner that had Katelyn in tears.

They passed by a tiny island, if you could call it that. It was no bigger than the kitchen in Katelyn's father's bungalow back in Evers. She found out later it was called Marriage Island. They stepped onto the island from a stone walkway that connected it to the side of the River Walk. The large tree that shaded the island was flanked on either side by two benches—one stone and one carved of wood—each engraved with a heart design on the top.

John pulled Katelyn to the island and sat her down. Laughter bubbled up inside her as he dropped to one knee and she knew. This was what he'd come down here to plan. He'd come to choose the right spot to ask her to marry him. And there was no way she wasn't saying yes. She loved this man with all her heart. He was her home. Her family.

John opened a small ring box and the solitaire diamond on the plain platinum band took Katelyn's breath away. It was exactly the ring she would have chosen for herself.

"I wish I'd been able to ask your father for his blessing before he went, but I'd like to think he'd approve," John said.

Katelyn smiled down at him as tears streamed down her face. She nodded. Her father would definitely approve.

"Katelyn, will you do me the honor of being my wife?" John asked and she smiled again at his formal manners. He may be a New Yorker, but somewhere along the way, he'd become a southern boy at heart.

"Yes," she said, and nodded again as she let laughter and tears flow freely. Her chest was so full of love and hope and peace. She knew with this man, with this love, she'd found her promise of forever.

Dɪᴅ you love seeing Sheriff John Davies fall? It's always the toughest of them that fall the hardest, don't you think? And I have to admit, I loved every minute of it!

Are you ready for Ashley and her man? I know, I know, me too! I've been waiting for Ashley to get her story from the minute she appeared on the page. Grab her book here. loriryanromance.com/book/Serve-and-protect

Let me know what you think!

Read on for chapter one of Serve and Protect!

CHAPTER ONE

Aꜱʜʟᴇʏ Wᴀʟᴋᴇʀ ʟᴏᴏᴋᴇᴅ out over the surface of the lake to where her siblings floated on inner tubes, a slow smile spreading on her face. She pressed her feet to the sun-warmed wood of the dock and let the heat soak into her skin. The day was perfect.

Well, that wasn't quite true.

Emma was two beats away from pushing Sam to his limit with her nagging, but that was a fairly normal state of affairs. Emma micromanaged. That's who she was. For the most part, all of the Walker siblings tuned her out when she got this way.

"I'm just saying, you could have handled it better." Emma's tone said there wasn't any "*just saying*" about it.

She flat-out thought she was right and she planned to make sure Sam knew it.

Sam growled at her. When push came to shove, he'd defend any of them to the end, but Emma walked all over his last nerve, then followed that up with a tap dance. "Carrie Ann knew damned well walking in that I wasn't looking for a relationship. It's not my problem she got buyer's remorse afterward. If she didn't want a one-night stand, she should have walked away the ten or so times I gave her the chance."

"She's your secretary!" The indignation in Emma's voice carried clear across the water. Their other brother, Nathan, was busy working his inner tube behind Sam, whose head lolled back, eyes closed as he appeared to relax in the sun, despite the argument with Emma. No doubt that was egging Emma on even more. She hated nothing more than being ignored.

Sam didn't answer, and Ashley had to agree with Emma a little. Sleeping with his secretary had been a bone-headed move. The woman clearly had *I want marriage and a family* stamped on her forehead, and now Sam had to work with her every day. But men were idiots. That was nothing new.

Ashley watched Nathan paddle, and knew he planned to dunk Sam. Nathan was the youngest of them all at twenty-two, and still the clown of the family. He also couldn't help trying to defuse the argument. But he was underestimating Sam. Ashley knew better. Just because his eyes were closed didn't mean you could take Sam out. You had to wait until that man was dead to the world asleep before trying a stunt like that.

She pressed her lips together, biting them to keep from laughing as she watched Sam's lips twitch the tiniest bit at the edges. Nathan paddled closer, using only the smallest movements of his hands to creep up on Sam. Emma seemed oblivious to Nathan's actions.

Sam turned suddenly and dove onto Nathan's tube, taking them both under the water together, and drenching Emma with the resulting splash. Her sister Cora had been smart enough to paddle slightly upstream to get herself out of the way. Ashley knew she was the smartest of them all for not going into the water with the boys to begin with.

She looked down at her tablet's screen and smiled. In truth, she had other reasons for not joining in the fun today. She had her own party going on online and didn't want to miss a second of it.

The cover of her latest book looked so good, she wanted to cry. Her cover artist had nailed it—from the colors, to the fonts, to the picture of the couple, to the size of her pen name. The bulging biceps of the male model encircled the woman protectively, but she was no mouse. She held a gun comfortably by her side as if it were an extension of her body, perfectly representing the heroine Ashley had penned. She never authored a heroine who was content to simply sit back and let the hero do all the fighting. And in her latest book, the heroine was every bit as well-trained and tough as the hero.

The water splashed when Cora pulled her tube up to

the dock, hanging onto the large rope ladder their dad had tied to the wood pylon years before. Cora leaned her head back as she shaded her eyes against the sun.

"How is the release going? Good so far?"

Cora was the only one who knew that Ashley was the person behind the pen name Leigh Dare. She hadn't really planned to keep the secret from her family and friends for so long. At first, when she'd decided to self-publish romantic suspense novels, she'd been afraid the books wouldn't sell. That she'd be a failure. So it had seemed like a good idea to let that failure be a private thing. And then, when her books had taken off, she'd been so stunned, she hadn't known what to do. Cora, of course, had figured it out. Cora was as avid a reader of romance novels as Ashley was. She'd read the books and spotted several phrases Ashley regularly used, and she'd figured it out by the third book.

Ashley smiled and nodded. "Yeah, people are posting that they love it so far. It's still surreal."

Watching hundreds of people congratulate her on the Leigh Dare Facebook page on her release day was still a dream. It still shocked her that anyone wanted to read her books. The fact that they loved them enough to contact her was unbelievable. Then, as people read the book, they posted their favorite quotes, or came on to tell her they loved it so far.

A few people had begun to tweet the links to their reviews. And those reviews raved about her latest hero and heroine. They loved the way Aiden Kane and Alexa Mayer played off one another. The way the sexual tension built until it exploded as they raced across the country, desperately trying to figure out who was trying to sabotage Dalton Chemical's latest research project.

Cora laughed. "Of course they do. The series is a huge hit, Ash. You're really good. Freakishly good, as a matter of fact," she said, pushing her feet lazily against the dock so that her tube bounced back and forth on the water.

Ashley grinned. "I am, aren't I?" She could say that to her sister because Cora was one of the few people who knew Ashley really wasn't as arrogant as her previous statement made her sound. Cora knew Ashley on a level no one else did. And she knew Ashley was incredibly humbled by her success in this new arena. Humbled and grateful beyond words, so she chose to go the tactless joke route instead.

Ashley's phone rang and she glanced at the screen before putting it back down. When Cora gave her that raised brow look that said *fess up*, Ashley rolled her eyes. They'd always had a weird ability to communicate, even though they weren't related by blood. When Ashley had first come to the Walkers as a foster child, she'd hated Cora. Resented her. In fact, at one time or another, all of the Walker children had been so at odds, no one would have thought they'd ever be as happy as they were now.

Within the first year, Cora had knocked down Ash's defenses. They were as different as night and day, both physically and in personality, but their bond was strong.

"It's Alice," she mumbled. Mumbling was not at all like Ashley. She spoke loud and clear and put out whatever she was feeling or thinking for the world's consumption. Without hesitation. Without censorship. But the recent calls from her former social worker, Alice Johnson—three of them in just as many days—made her want to close in on herself.

Cora's forehead wrinkled up. "Ah. I get it," she said after a moment. "It's almost your anniversary."

Ashley pressed her lips together and nodded. "I just don't want to revisit it this year, you know? She hasn't called the past few years, so I'm not entirely sure that's why she's calling now, but I just, well, you know."

Cora did know. None of the Walker kids wanted to be reminded of the reasons they had become Walkers in the first place. Their pasts weren't fun, by any means. But they were all happy to be Walkers now. Theirs was a family truly built on love. Blood, sweat, tears, and love. They celebrated that, having moved past their backgrounds, for the most part. But sometimes their former social workers thought about them around their "anniversary dates" and got in touch. Ashley was fairly sure they didn't even do it consciously. They wouldn't ever seek to hurt the kids they'd helped. But as much as they were all grateful to the people who had helped them get out of the situations they'd been in, they weren't eager to revisit those times.

"Maybe she's figured out your secret and wants to congratulate the next *New York Times* bestselling author," Cora said with a grin.

Ashley laughed, with a glance to her siblings to be sure they were far enough away they didn't overhear Cora.

"Yeah, maybe you're right. It's probably not related to my anniversary date at all. I'll call her," she said, dismissing the alert on her phone that told her she had a new voicemail. "But not until we get back. I just want to relax for now."

Now it was Cora's turn to laugh. "You mean watch your book's rank obsessively, read every blog post or review posted, and stalk your favorite readers online to see if they mention *Dead Run* in any comments or posts?"

Ashley grinned. "Exactly. Relax."

She grabbed the reading glasses that sat near her Kindle —this pair hot pink with white temples—and shoved her feet back into her flip-flops. She stood and shaded her eyes, looking down at Cora, who still bobbed on the gentle waters of the lake. Emma and Sam still fought in the background, and she could hear Nathan joking around, trying to distract the pair.

"It's my turn to cook," she said as she looked toward the lake house that was her family's vacation home. It was only twenty minutes away from their home in Evers, Texas, and it was more a rustic cabin than lake house, with a kitchen, open common room, and two bedrooms, but it was all theirs. Their parents had the master bedroom and all five kids still bunked in the other bedroom, drawing straws over the two sets of bunk beds and one full bed that took up the entire floor space of the room. It wasn't anything to brag about, but it was a treasured family haven.

Cora wrinkled her nose. "Foil meals or baked spaghetti?"

"Foil meals," Ashley answered with a grin. She was the

only one in her family who still stuck to the two meals she'd learned how to make as a teen. Everyone else had managed to add to their repertoire, but she loved the comfort of the meals her mom had taught her to make. They were camping staples, and to her, camping staples were what their time at the lake house called for.

Cora laughed and shoved off from the dock to rejoin the rest of their family floating several yards away. Ashley waved to the group and then headed up to the kitchen to start cooking. With any luck, her mom would be there and they could chat while Ashley got dinner going. Besides, her mom made a much better salad than Ashley did. Her siblings would be happier with dinner if her mom had a hand in it.

GARRET HENSLEY WALKED into the station house and tossed his gym bag onto the warped surface of his desk. The place didn't exactly scream *modern*, and lately, he'd felt a bit like his body was going the way of the station house. He kept in shape, so it wasn't so much that as it was the lack of stimulation. The lack of anything other than work in his life. It wasn't like he got out much or socialized with anyone who didn't wear a badge or work in a crime lab. People who didn't know the smell of a dead body or what it was like to chase down a junkie intent on slipping from your grasp.

That hadn't bothered him much in the past, but lately, he'd begun to notice. Hensley had been one of six detective sergeants in the Branson Falls Criminal Investigations Division for five years. He loved the work, but his life was stagnant—empty, somehow. And for some unknown reason, he felt a hell of a lot older than his thirty-three years.

He ran a hand down his face and looked around the bullpen at the desks of the other detectives and the two animal services officers who also shared the space. They all had the look of people who'd been overworked and underpaid for far too long. Of men and women who'd spent a few too many hours inside. Well, that wasn't entirely true. The animal services officers had tans.

At least he had kept his physique, Garret thought as he eyed the guts forming on the frames of two of the men taking up space at the desks across from him. He hit the gym or ran every morning without fail. He wouldn't give in to the temptation to place his sleep over his physical fitness. Not when he'd had to give up healthy eating due to the demands of a job that had him dining from a takeout bag at the drive-through more often than not. The least he could do each day was run the calories off, even when the job kept his sleeping hours to a minimum.

There was a needling thought at the back of his mind that his life needed to change, but he pushed it aside. He'd been doing this a long time. It was what he knew. The detectives of the CID covered crimes, from robbery, assault, up to homicide for Branson Falls and the surrounding towns for miles. They often had to drive an hour or more to investigate crimes on limited resources and a shoestring budget. It wasn't a job someone did for money or luxuries.

In fact, Garret wasn't entirely sure why he did the job anymore. But that thought would have to wait. His captain stood in the doorway to his office, and barked, "Hensley!" His standard call to action when they'd caught a case. Garret's partner, Doug Mann, wasn't in the bullpen yet. He'd get the info from the captain, then rustle up Doug and head out. Knowing Doug, the older man was probably in the can with his morning paper. Doug was pretty committed to his morning ritual. Another thing Garret was purposefully ignoring was Doug's upcoming retirement. In six months he'd be breaking in a new partner and saying goodbye to the man who'd had his back in more ways than he could count for years.

Captain Sharp had lowered his six-foot-four frame into the creaking wooden chair behind the government-issue metal desk that took up most of his office. He didn't look up as he rattled off Garret's assignment.

"One-eight-seven at the apartments over on Guadalupe." *Homicide.*

Garret was glad Sharp hadn't looked up. He didn't catch the way Garret's body swayed at his words. A homicide at the apartment building where Garret grew up. The building where Alice Johnson—a woman who was more mother to him than his own had ever been—lived. He put a hand on the back of the chair in front of the desk and gripped it. Hard.

He hadn't known his father—other than to know the Irish spelling of Garret's name had come courtesy of his father's Irish roots, which as an adult had struck him as odd, since his mother had given him her British last name. He'd buried his mother when he was nineteen, and other than a few aunts and uncles he never saw, Alice was the only thing resembling family he had left in this world.

"Got a number?" *Please not 207. Please God.* Even to know she was close to violence like that would be too much. But if it were her... No, *that* he couldn't handle.

His Captain read from the notepad by his phone. "Two—"

God, please, no. Please. His hands gripped, squeezing the crap out of the back of the chair in an effort to—well, he didn't know what. To ward off the blow? How could he possibly do that? There was no way to ward off what was coming.

"Oh-seven."

Get Serve and Protect now! loriryanromance.com/book/Serve-and-protect

To my wonderful husband for his patience and support. It's truly a wonder that you put up with me. No, really. Truly.

Thank you to Susan Smith and Kate Baray for brainstorming the plot over and over with me, and to my critique groups for reading bits and pieces and helping to shape the characters and the story. Thank you to the many editors who worked on this book with me, both in its first incarnation as Everlasting, and in the current version. You keep me out of trouble!

A big thank you to my beta readers, law enforcement officers, and mental health experts who consulted on the criminal and medical aspects of this story. Your input, as always, was invaluable: Bette Hansen, Chief Scott Silverii, PhD, Officer Julianne Brewer, and Dr. Ashley B. Hampton.

Thank you to Patricia Parent and to my mom, my final set of eyes, for cleaning up after me. Thank you to all the friends and friends-of-friends who read the pre-release version for me. I owe you all so much.

ABOUT THE AUTHOR

Lori Ryan is a NY Times and USA Today bestselling author who writes romantic suspense, contemporary romance, and sports romance. She lives with an extremely understanding husband, three wonderful children, and two mostly-behaved dogs in Austin, Texas. It's a bit of a zoo, but she wouldn't change a thing.

Lori published her first novel in April of 2013 and hasn't looked back since then. She loves to connect with her readers.

For new release info and bonus content, join her newslettter here: loriryanromance.com/lets-keep-touch.

Follow her online:

facebook.com/loriryanromance

twitter.com/Loriryanauthor

instagram.com/loriryanauthor

Made in the USA
Columbia, SC
22 June 2021